LINUS

CHRISTMAS SPRITES
BOOK 4

MACY BLAKE

Linus

Cover by A.J. Corza, alexandriacorza.com

Edited by Stacy Sirkel

Formatted by Stacy Sirkel

SYNOPSIS

Never sleigh never.

Linus is having a Christ-*massive* problem. His cousins have all found their fated mates and their sprite magic is making beautiful things happen in the small town of Mistletoe Falls they call home. His magic? Well, it's making a fa-la-la-la-lasting impression...and not in a good way.

No need to Claus a scene!

When Colby's best friend runs away to Mistletoe Falls, Colby follows. From the moment he arrives, things are an *elf*-ing mess. Strange things keep occurring in and around the Tinseled Inn, all involving its bewitching owner, Linus. Colby is determined to find out Linus's secret, and if he doesn't end up getting his chestnuts roasted, he may discover that Linus will make more than his Christmas bright.

If you love fated mates, Christmas hijinks, and magical elves, er, sprites, who make the season bright, this holiday romance will help you have a tree-mendous holiday season.

1

COLBY

T hwack. *Thwack. Thwack.*

Someone was going to die.

Colby's pounding head matched the rhythm of the banging coming from somewhere in the Tinseled Inn. His misadventures with energy drinks on the drive to town had left him with a massive headache and a sleep schedule that didn't know if it was day or night.

He flung back the covers and shot a glare at the life-sized nutcrackers flanking the fireplace of his best friend's room at the Inn, half convinced the horrific banging noise was coming from them. They weren't moving however, so whatever evil he needed to destroy had to be somewhere else.

As Colby left the room, he reminded himself with each step that as a licensed attorney, murder would be a very bad move for his career.

Thwack. Thwack. Thwack.

Even if the noise made him forget all rational thought. He followed the sound with one hand on his head. The Inn seemed to grow like that freaky hall in *The Shining*. No matter how many rooms he wandered through, he couldn't find anyone to make it stop.

"What is that noise?" Colby bellowed into the Inn.

His voice echoed around him.

It wasn't creepy at all.

Considering the thwacks continued, Colby followed the sound toward the back of the Inn. He avoided all doors in fear of Jack Nicholson suddenly appearing to shout, *"Here's Johnny!"*

Instead, he found a man wearing a red cardigan sweater covered in tiny white snowflakes in the backyard of the Inn. He seemed to be trying to chop down a tree, if the axe in his hand was any indication. Not that Colby could see any cut marks on said tree, which confused him even further.

"Stop it!"

For a second, Colby thought he was the one who'd yelled, but no, the man stopped swinging the axe to bellow at a group of squirrels sitting on a branch in the very tree he was walloping with the axe. The squirrels appeared to be pelting the guy with acorns while chittering angrily at him.

The guy swung the axe again, but somehow managed to not do any damage to the tree. It wasn't really a surprise considering his swing was terrible and his grip was...well, the fact that the axe hadn't gone flying was likely due to some miracle.

Colby couldn't even process what he was seeing as the man lifted the axe and wiggled his hips as he prepared to take another swing. "What. Are. You. *DOING*?"

Red sweater man shrieked and spun around, nearly dropped the axe on his foot in the process. His bright blue eyes widened. "Who are you?"

Colby ran forward and took the axe from his hands before disaster struck. "My name is Colby Russell. And you are?"

"Um, Linus. Of course. What a silly question. Can you give me my axe back?" Linus glanced up at him with those big baby blues, but Colby's years of practicing law made him immune to innocent looks.

"I don't think so. Linus, what exactly are you trying to do here?"

Linus looked at Colby like he had less than two brain cells to rub together. He rubbed his fingers through his ginger-red beard before answering. "Trying to cut down a tree."

Linus said the words *very* slowly, as if that would help Colby understand them better.

It didn't.

"Have you ever used an axe before in your life?"

Linus scowled. "What's it to you?"

Colby's temple began to pulse. He probably had a vein popping out on his forehead. "Okay, let's try again. What exactly are you trying to *accomplish* here Linus?"

"I'm trying to cut down a tree," Linus said, even more slowly than before.

This time he added the miming action of swinging the axe, as if that might help.

It didn't.

Colby's eyelid began to flutter along with the twitch in his temple. "*Why?*"

"Um, firewood. Of course."

"Of course," Colby said. "You do realize that if you cut this tree down, it's more than likely going to fall on the Inn."

"It most certainly—"

Colby pointed to the angle where Linus had been attempting to chop, then drew a straight line in the air to the roof of the Inn. "—will land right about there."

Linus huffed.

"Why are you cutting this tree down anyway? It looks good."

"Firewood. Honestly, don't you listen?"

Colby pinched the bridge of his nose, wishing he could just bellow for Tate to come fix this. "And do you expect this firewood to be used soon?"

"Maybe." Linus drew the word out and Colby twitched again. "You ask the strangest questions."

"Linus, wood needs to be seasoned first, which will take up to a year. Green wood isn't great to burn. It has to have time to dry out."

"Dag nab it." Linus stomped his foot. "Are you sure?"

"I'm positive. I'm sure there's a place nearby that sells cords of wood," Colby offered. "It'll save you a ton of work, and the Inn's owner a huge insurance claim. I suggest you take the easy route and buy what you need."

Linus gave him another look that suggested Colby was dumber than a box of rocks. "I *am* the Inn's owner. One of them, anyway."

A lightbulb finally went off, and Colby began to understand what was going on. Probably due to the peace and quiet now that the thwacking had stopped. "You're one of Eldon's cousins?"

Linus narrowed his eyes, causing the little white ball on the Santa hat he wore to fall into his face. Colby hadn't noticed the hat over the brightness of the sweater. Or maybe it was because of his twitching eye. Probably both.

"You know Eldon?"

"Well, I know Tate. I'm his best friend. I came in yesterday. Or was it the day before? I'm a bit confused at the moment."

"*Clearly.* Where are you staying?" Linus asked innocently as he began to slowly stretch his hand toward the axe.

Colby took a step back, taking the axe with him as he gave what he'd been assured was a very intimidating lawyer glare at Linus. He'd had witnesses crumble under the power of that look.

Linus didn't seem even remotely bothered.

"Here. I slept in Tate's room last night." Colby glanced at his watch. "Well, most of today. My hours are a little messed up at the moment."

"Hmph." Linus looked at the axe, clearly dreaming up something diabolical, unaffected by Colby's best fear-inducing scowl. "Can you drive?"

The question was so unexpected Colby simply blinked at Linus.

Linus stepped closer and looked at him. "Is something...*wrong* with you? Maybe I should call Tate. Do you need a doctor?"

Colby growled. "Why does everyone in this town keep asking me that? No, nothing is *wrong* with me. And yes, I can drive. Of course I can drive."

"Oh good. Then you can drive me out to Weston's Tree Farm. They'll have firewood."

"I can drive...what? Why would I do that?"

"Because I'm banned from driving due to one or twelve unfortunate accidents. Come on. We'll take Oberon's truck. It ought to fit enough wood for what I need."

Colby found himself following Linus even though he wasn't entirely sure why. "Aren't the fireplaces in the Inn gas? The one in Tate's room is."

Linus grabbed a set of keys out of a small cabinet by the back door. "Yes. Why?"

Colby scratched his head, wondering if he was still asleep. "So why do you need firewood?"

"For the pyre, obviously. Come on, Colby. I need a lift. Help a guy out in his time of need."

Against his better judgement, Colby followed Linus to the carriage house behind the Inn where a perfectly restored antique truck sat. Its gleaming red paint shone in the afternoon sun. Colby's heart fluttered at its beauty.

"Here," Linus said, tossing the keys to Colby. "Drive."

"I can't drive—" Colby caught the keys while he spoke, but Linus's outburst cut him off.

"You *said* you could *drive!*" Linus flung his hands up in the air.

"—someone's vehicle without their permission," Colby continued, ignoring Linus's outburst. Especially one as perfect as this.

Linus let out a long, pained sigh. He pulled a cell phone from his pocket and pulled up his contacts. Moments later the phone began to ring. Linus put the phone on speaker.

"Hey, Linus. What's up?"

"Oberon, do you mind if Tate's best friend Colby uses your truck to drive me out to Weston's for some firewood? He's making me ask permission like I'm twelve and wouldn't be allowed to borrow my own cousin's truck."

"You aren't the one driving?" Oberon asked.

Colby immediately approved of Oberon. A very wise man.

"No, Colby is."

"Then sure. Go for it."

Damn it. Maybe Oberon wasn't so wise after all. Why would he let a stranger drive his obviously precious truck.

"Linus," Oberon continued, "why do you—"

"Thanks, Obie!" Linus hung up the phone. "There. *Now* will you drive me?"

"Sure." Colby climbed into the truck, admiring the heavy weight of the metal door as it swung shut. He ran his hand over the perfectly restored vintage steering wheel.

The temptation to actually get a chance to drive the beauty overran any impulse to deny Linus the trip. It would take a little getting used to, no doubt, with its unique gear shift, but he'd never driven a truck quite like this and really couldn't resist the chance.

With a turn of the key, the truck rumbled to life. Colby might have shivered a little in excitement. Not that he would confess that little piece of information to a soul.

Linus ruined the moment by making a little scoffing noise.

Colby shot Linus another stern look. "This truck doesn't move until your seatbelt is on."

Linus muttered several words under his breath, but he reached for the seatbelt and got it buckled. "*Happy?*"

"Ecstatic. Which way to Weston's Tree Farm?"

"Um..." Linus looked left, then right, a puzzled frown forming on his face. "That way!"

"Are you sure?"

"I've lived here my entire life, Colby. I'm absolutely positive."

Linus was absolutely wrong.

It took them four tries to find the farm. Only four because Colby finally stopped at a gas station to ask for directions.

By the time they reached the tree farm, Colby's headache had returned in full force. He wanted nothing more than a hot meal and something to make his head stop pounding.

Instead, he found himself in a packed parking lot where several people wearing bright red aprons helped customers load Christmas trees onto the top or into the back of vehicles. With only a couple of weeks to the big day, it seemed to be high season for Weston's.

A young guy wearing a red and black flannel shirt under his apron approached the truck, looking puzzled at Colby's position behind the wheel.

Colby rolled down the window and smiled what he hoped was a friendly smile. In a complete reversal of the reaction he usually received from people, residents of Mistletoe Falls hadn't exactly been welcoming to him. He wasn't sure if it was his smile or some-thing else.

Luckily, the guy saw Linus and grinned, ignoring Colby completely. "Linus! I wasn't expecting you back again this season. You didn't have a problem with your tree, did you?"

"It's perfect as always, West. I'm looking for some...what was that word, Colby?"

"Cords."

"Right, cords of firewood. Do you happen to have some?"

"Sure. Out by the barn. Get what you need, and we'll settle up when you're done."

"Thanks!"

With a wave, West wandered over to the next customer while Linus pointed at a big red barn in the distance. "The barn," Linus said.

"Yeah, I got that." Colby put the truck into gear and began driving.

"*Yeah, I got that,*" Linus muttered under his breath. "*And I can drive and be cranky and scowly. And I don't have a major life crisis to deal with, unlike some people. Meh meh meh.*"

"You do realize I can hear you, right?"

Linus sniffed. "There's the firewood."

Colby drove the truck next to the neatly stacked cords and stopped. Linus hopped out and began throwing bundles into the back of the truck with careless abandon. Colby winced at the potential damage to the paint job but he was more worried about the frenzied pace Linus used to add to the growing pile in the back.

"Exactly how much wood do you need?" Colby asked.

"I'm not sure. A lot." Linus continued to toss bundles into the back before he paused and looked at Colby. "You just going to stand there or...."

"You know, I could be on a beautiful, snowy slope in Colorado right now, being waited on hand and foot and spoiled rotten by Tate's mom. But no, I think I have to be the hero and save him from himself, only to have everyone in his supposedly cheerful town accuse me of being weird and on drugs, all while bossing me around."

Colby heaved a cord into the back of the truck.

"Well, there's no need to throw a *tantrum* about it," Linus said. "I only asked for a little help."

"Asked? You *asked*? No, Linus, you haven't asked a thing."

"Semantics. You clearly need some rest. You're awfully cranky for someone who spent the entire day in bed. Was the room not comfortable? The bed too soft? The pillows too fluffy? You look like the kind of guy who needs a little extra back support."

Colby closed his eyes and breathed in through his nose, then out through his mouth. He did it for a count of ten before opening his eyes. Linus stood there staring at him.

"I think you have enough firewood," Colby said through clenched teeth. His relaxation technique hadn't worked.

At all.

Besides, the bed of the truck was half full and his patience was empty.

Linus eyed it speculatively. "It'll be a good start. Besides, I should probably get you back to town. Maybe ask Dr. Lane to take a look at you."

"I don't need a doctor," Colby barked.

"Oh, don't worry. Miles is a vet. But he can probably help. You growl a lot for a human."

Colby started the truck, glared until Linus buckled his seatbelt, then drove them back into town.

When they reached the Inn—without getting lost this time due to Colby's superior sense of direction—Tate, Eldon, and a few other men Colby didn't recognize stood outside waiting for them.

Colby didn't bother offering to help unload. He hurried to Tate and dropped to one knee in front of his best friend since he was five years old. "Please, feed me and give me something to make the headache stop. Then tell me again why I have to stay here because I'm pretty sure this place has some bad juju. I don't like it. It's scary and I need snow. Or a beach in the Caribbean. Anything but the Overlook. Nurse Ratched is gonna come for me any second."

Tate helped Colby up, giving him a look not too different from the ones Linus had been giving him for the past few hours. "Whoa. Mixing your Jack Nicholson movie metaphors. Must be low blood sugar. I can take you to Carol's—"

"No! She hates me."

Eldon moved to Colby's side and dropped an arm around his shoulders. "I think you've just had a rough couple of days. Let's see what we have inside and get you something for that headache. Obie, put the kettle on, would you?"

"Sure."

"I have some fresh baked bran muffins. I'll get them out."

"Bran—" Colby's protest was cut off by Tate's finger over his lips.

"Thank you, Nyall. That's very sweet of you. Let's just sit quietly and relax. Eldon, do you know where there's some painkillers around here? Pretty sure he has a migraine coming on. His eye is twitching, and his pulse is throbbing in his temple. Never a good sign."

They hustled Colby into a chair in the kitchen. Then one of the guys sat down next to him and put his fingers on Colby's wrist.

"I'm being checked out by a vet, aren't I?" Colby dropped his head onto the table. The thud echoed through the room.

"Is he usually this over-wrought?" The vet seemed concerned, which didn't bode well for Colby.

"Only when he hasn't been fed and watered. It's in the care and feeding of Colby manual. I haven't had a chance to share it with you yet."

Colby lifted his head. "There's not a manual."

Tate had his phone out and a second later, everyone's phone dinged with a message. "No. Not a manual at all. Nope."

Colby thumped his head back onto the table. Maybe he was in the Cuckoo's Nest after all.

2

LINUS

The next morning, Linus stood in the backyard with his phone in one hand and a few cords of wood on the ground beside him. "Okay, log cabin, inverse, lean to, or star. *Hmm.* The star is appropriate symbolically, but it's less than impressive."

"Are you talking to yourself?"

Linus shrieked and spun around to find Colby standing at the back door staring at him. "Must you sneak up on me?

"I cleared my throat. Twice."

Linus doubted it. He would have heard. Probably. "Hmph. What can I do for you?"

"I was hoping for some breakfast. The little card in the room says breakfast is between seven and nine. It's only eight-thirty."

"Oh, right. Of course."

"You say 'of course' a lot," Colby said.

"And that's a problem *because?*"

"It's not. I noticed, that's all."

"Well, I hope you're feeling better. You were quite the sight yesterday afternoon. Miles was concerned."

"Yeah, note to self, no more energy drinks for me. I lost two days to those things. Plus, I needed a vet to take care of me. Not one of my best days."

"What you need is some of my cocoa."

Colby perked up at the suggestion. "With those little marsh-mallows?"

"Are you sure you're some big wig lawyer? Tate said you're wicked smart."

"And that's a problem *because?*"

The teasing glint in Colby's eyes at his mimicked question from earlier made Linus snicker.

"It's not. Extra marshmallows for the big, bad lawyer. Now, I happen to have made a delicious quiche this morning, and Nyall brought over some crusty bread that is magical with my special butter. I think a good meal will sort out the rest of that poison you drank to get here."

"That sounds perfect."

"Good," Linus said. "Normally, I serve guests in the dining room, but I suppose you're close enough to family that you can sit in here with me if you'd like."

"I'd like that." Colby sank down in one of the chairs, looking around the room with a little grin as he did.

Linus bustled around the kitchen preparing Colby's breakfast, checking on his newest guest with quick glances while he did. At least the poor thing had a little more color. He'd obviously gotten a good night's sleep. After a hearty breakfast, Colby should be good as new.

When Linus placed the plate in front of Colby, Colby grinned up at him. "This looks great."

Linus couldn't help but smile in return. Colby's smiles were much better than his snarly scowls from the day before. A small thump sounded behind him, and Linus turned to see his kitchen garland drooping yet again.

He bit back a curse and fixed Colby a cup of cocoa with extra marshmallows. After he handed it over, Linus dragged a ladder out of the pantry. Setting it up near the fallen section, he stomped his way up the rungs and reached for the greenery.

He'd almost managed to reach the hook when the ladder wobbled. Linus grabbed the cabinet, but to his horror, the ladder kept moving. He saw a very painful landing in his future. But instead of hitting the ground, he landed on something else. Something that wasn't the ground or the counter.

Linus opened his eyes and found himself cradled in Colby's arms. "How did you...."

"What were you doing on the ladder without a spotter? Linus! That's not safe!"

Linus poked Colby in the pec. "Wow, you're *really* strong. Much stronger than you look."

Colby sighed and lowered Linus to his feet. He put both of his hands on Linus's shoulders and looked into his eyes. Colby's eyes were pale gray, kinda stormy actually, and he'd not bothered shaving in the few days since he arrived. He looked like a ruffian.

Linus adored ruffians.

"*Linus*, pay attention."

"I am. Blah blah ladders. Blah blah safety."

Colby shook his head. "It's not even nine in the morning, and I want a drink."

"Well, as long as it isn't one of those energy drinks. They turn you into a monster."

Colby turned to go back to the table but froze when he caught a glimpse of Linus's creation through the kitchen window. "What exactly are you doing out there? You realize you can't light a fire that close to the inn, right?"

Linus scoffed. "Light a fire. As if I would ever...so how far away does it need to be...hypothetically speaking, of course?"

Colby ran his hand over his face. "Linus, you can't start a fire in a residential neighborhood without multiple safety measures in place first. You might even need a permit. Think of all the homes you'd be putting at risk."

Linus drummed his fingers against the counter. He needed a pyre, and he needed it stat. All of his decorations were falling apart. He had to have done something to upset the goddesses or fate or whatever, because if there was one thing Linus was an expert at, it was holiday decor.

People came from miles around to simply stay at the Tinseled Inn and admire his themed rooms. But now, his garland was falling.

His garland.

Falling.

It was horrible.

To make matters worse, all of his cousins had found their fated mates and their sprite magic had become this amazing thing of beauty, but his garland went kaput.

He must have done something to affect his standing with the goddesses to deserve such a punishment. He needed to offer them gifts or a sacrifice or something to get back into their good standing.

Hence, the pyre.

"Maybe I'll go with the star after all. But the log cabin really had potential."

"What?"

"Oh, nothing."

"Linus, please tell me you aren't going to light a fire."

Linus thought fast. He really hated to lie, but considering Colby's human status, he couldn't exactly tell the truth. "I'm...going to put one of those electrical logs out there. Not everyone celebrates holidays the same way, Colby. We try to be inclusive here in Mistletoe Falls."

"Electrical logs?"

"It's symbolic of Yule."

Colby looked very confused. Not that Linus could blame him since he was making the whole thing up. Well, sort of. He *was* building a pyre for symbolic reasons, and it *was* connected to Yule.

So, it wasn't a lie so much as stretching the truth. Linus was sure, as a lawyer, Colby would appreciate the difference.

"That's really nice of you," Colby said. "After I finish eating, I'll help you get it set up. We'll have to run an extension cord out there."

"Yep," Linus said.

Dag nab it. He'd hoped Colby would head off to find Tate in his studio or something. Although he and Eldon likely canoodling somewhere considering their newly mated status and all.

Linus sighed.

He wished he was newly mated.

While Colby ate, Linus glanced under the kitchen sink and made sure the fire extinguisher was in place. Not that he'd need it. He planned on being very safe...when Colby wasn't looking.

After Colby finished eating, he followed Linus outside and they looked at the images of pyres that Linus found on the internet. They discussed their options, and Colby agreed that the log cabin style set up would make the nicest looking log stack for the "fake" Yule pyre.

They spent several hours making a beautifully square-shaped pyre that stood nearly as tall as Linus.

Oh, the goddesses would be pleased.

Then Colby helped him run an extension cord and set up the fake fire log thing Linus dug out of a corner of the attic. All Linus would have to do is pull the thing back out when the time came and *voila*! Sacrificial pyre for the goddesses to beg forgiveness. Then he'd get his mate and all's well that ends well. Done and dusted.

"You know," Colby said, stepping back and eyeing their creation. "We should probably add some kindling. It'll make it look more real."

"Kindling." Linus frowned and pulled out his phone.

"You know," Colby said. "The smaller sticks and branches that start the fire. What are you looking up? Don't you know what kindling is?"

Linus scoffed. "*Of course* I know what kindling is. I was, um, looking up its etymology. Kin-*dling*. *Kind*-ling. It's a weird word. I want to know where it comes from. And look, Old Norse to Middle English. Isn't that *fascinating*?"

Colby didn't seem convinced if the blank stare he gave Linus was any indication.

"Some of us are interested in how the world works, *Colby*. Culture is all around us if only we pause and take a moment to look."

"You're up to something. Why don't you save us both some time and tell me what it is?"

"Oh, look at the time. I need to go get lunch started for the guests. Busy busy. An Inn owner's work is never done. Ta ta!"

Linus's escape effort didn't work. Colby simply followed him back into the kitchen.

"I could eat," Colby said, sitting down at the kitchen table. "I did haul logs for you. It seems only fair that you feed me."

It did seem fair.

Dag nab it.

Although Linus was also a bit noshy now that he thought about it. He'd made a delicious chicken salad the night before with leftover roast chicken he'd prepared for the guests who'd chosen to dine at the Inn. With fresh croissants from Nyall and a nice fruit salad, it made the perfect lunch for guests on the go.

And since it wasn't particularly cold outside, Linus didn't feel the need to get out one of his many containers of frozen soup. He cooked huge batches of it in the fall, then froze it for occasions like this. It made his life easier on those cold days when a nice hot soup made all the difference.

Colby seemed quiet as they ate, and he didn't glare at Linus even once.

It became a bit creepy after a few minutes. "You okay?"

"Hmm? Oh, yeah. This is really good, by the way. I'm thinking about what I need to do to actually be able to stay in Mistletoe Falls with Tate through the end of the year like he wants. I appreciate Aaron giving up his room for me, but I'll also need to find a place to set up a mini-office. There isn't a lot that I'll have to do over the next few weeks, but I have some work that can't be put off."

"I can help with that," Linus said. "It'll involve moving a little furniture but considering your big catch-Linus-from-a-falling-ladder muscles, I don't think it'll be a problem."

"You do realize I only broke your fall because I was a foot away from you, right?"

"Yeah, but you could have dropped me. Hell, I could have landed on you and broken something. I'm already worried about your back."

"My back is fine," Colby said. "Promise."

"Well, I'm still thinking about taking that mattress topper off your bed to see if it helps."

Colby groaned and dropped his head into his hand. Linus grinned but hid it before Colby looked up again.

"What kind of furniture?"

"Mainly a desk. I have a gorgeous antique secretary on the second floor we could bring down. It's not a big fancy lawyer desk, but it'll work."

"I only need a spot for my laptop."

Linus grinned. "Come on. Let me show you the room."

After making sure Colby followed, Linus led the way from the kitchen, through both the dining room and formal living room. A small room they occasionally used for private events like family dinners sat off the formal living room.

"It used to be the parlor and music room," Linus explained as he opened the door. The multiple windows allowed light to flood the room, making it bright and cheerful even on a dull, cloudy day.

Oddly enough, Linus had chosen to decorate the seldom-used spaced in smokey blues and champagne. The blue kind of matched Colby's eyes. What a coincidence.

Colby looked around the room and nodded his approval. "And you're sure you don't mind if I take it over for a couple weeks?"

"Not at all. There's a powder room next door, and you know where the kitchen is. If you're planning on staying, we might as well make you feel at home."

"Thank you, Linus. That's really kind of you."

"Pfft," Linus waved off the praise and eyed the room. "I'll get it all set up for you on *one* condition."

Colby groaned. "I was waiting on the condition."

"You have to help me gather some kindling. It's only fair since you brought it up."

Colby shook his head and laughed. "Fine. Is there a park or a small patch of woods nearby?"

Linus nodded. "I have some big bags we can use, too. It'll be a delightful afternoon adventure. A little fresh air will be good for you."

Colby chuckled and his eyes got a strange twinkle in them.

"That look means you're up to something," Linus said.

"I'm just laughing. Afternoon delight. I don't think that means what you think it means."

Linus frowned. "You really are a weird man. Speaking of strange, didn't you bring anything more appropriate to wear? Some nice sweaters, perhaps?"

"I'm not a sweater kind of guy, Linus."

Linus gasped. "*Colby*. Every man is a sweater kind of guy. Are you so uncouth?"

"Apparently so."

"Well, I'll just have to remedy that. I swear, I have to do everything around here. Next thing you know, I'll be reviewing those contracts for you too. You go get changed into something more weather appropriate while I make us a nice bottle of cocoa to take on our adventure."

Colby didn't move, so Linus shooed him out the door and up the stairs. Poor thing really seemed out of sorts. Linus would have to have a talk with Tate about it. If they needed to get him to see a doctor, it would be wise to do it in the next few days before everyone began taking time off for the holidays.

When he returned a few minutes later, Colby had added a leather jacket over the hoodie he'd been wearing earlier. The entire ensemble was black.

"I'm going to start calling you Wednesday," Colby said.

Colby frowned. "Why?"

"Because you're dressed like you're going to a funeral. Don't you have anything holiday appropriate?"

Colby crossed his arms over his chest and glared. "Do you want my help or not?"

Linus sighed. "I want your help. I'm simply pointing out that Mistletoe Falls is not an all-black kind of place. Dress for the job you want and all that."

"I don't want a job in Mistletoe Falls," Colby said.

Linus shoved the big blue plastic bags he'd picked up at a giant retailer against Colby's chest. "It's an *expression*, Colby. You take everything so seriously. We definitely have some room for improvement."

"Oh *we* do, do we?"

"Absolutely. We've got time, though. I've had harder nuts to crack than you."

"Harder...you know what, I'm not going to touch that one."

"What?"

"Nothing, Linus. Where are we going?"

"Have you forgotten already? Honestly, Colby, I think we should have you checked out."

Colby sighed. "I meant, where *exactly* are we going, Linus. I know we're going to gather kindling. But where?"

"Oh. A couple blocks down from the Inn. Where else? There are two empty lots loaded with trees. I think we'll find what we need there. We can always get a little more from the trees behind the Tinseled Inn, but I really think a brisk walk and some fresh air would be good for you."

"I had plenty of fresh air hauling logs this morning."

"Gosh, you're such a cranky thing. Don't you think it would be nice to *branch* out this holiday season?"

Colby smirked. "Or maybe you need to *lighten* up."

Linus stopped dead in his tracks and stared. "You punned me. Oh, this is good news. There's hope for you yet. Not a lot of hope, mind you, but a little."

Colby really could do with a little sprucing up of his holiday spirit, and Linus was just the sprite for the job.

Once he dealt with the sacrifice for the goddesses, that is.

3

COLBY

C olby had faced many intense negotiations since he'd become a corporate lawyer. He'd walked into rooms, knowing his position was weaker, but still walked out ahead.

So why were his knees trembling when Tate dragged him into Carol's and Crepes for lunch the next day? They didn't *need* to go out to lunch. Linus had offered Colby lunch at the Inn. And they'd all gathered around the kitchen table for a nice dinner the night before after he and Linus had gathered kindling. There was absolutely zero need to go to Carol's for lunch.

"You're being ridiculous," Tate said as they entered the diner.

Tate headed straight for a small table in the front window, completely ignoring the *please wait to be seated* sign. Colby followed but looked around the diner for Carol first to make sure he wasn't going to get in trouble.

Colby didn't see her, though, so he took the seat across from Tate and yawned. "I've drafted a few contracts for you to look over before we set up a meeting with your parents. Read through them this afternoon and let me know what you want me to change."

Tate stared at him for a minute before being interrupted by a waitress carrying a tray to their table. She put plates in front of both of them along with glasses of water.

"Thanks, Tracy."

Colby blinked down at his plate. "Did we order? I don't think we ordered."

"Nobody orders. We all get the special."

"What if you don't like the special?"

Tate sighed. "Colby, it's an opened-faced turkey sandwich with a big pile of fluffy mashed potatoes. What's not to like?"

"Point."

"So eat. And why are you yawning? You've been sleeping a lot."

"I don't know. Its the strangest thing." Colby looked up at Tate and grinned. "Probably need the rest after all the parties I had to attend without you last week."

Tate snorted. "I'd feel sorry for you, but I just can't. I've been to those parties. They aren't that bad."

"Yeah, well, you didn't have to keep Greg out of trouble. Your brother is a menace."

"Hmm."

"What's that mean?"

"Is he though?" Tate asked, his expression serious. "Or has he never had a chance?"

Colby pondered the question as he took his first bite of food. He quickly went in for a second before answering. "A little of both. Why? You thinking Greg should be the heir to the kingdom instead of you?"

"He wants it," Tate said.

"But he doesn't have the Tatum touch, and do not smirk like I said something filthy. I could be referring to your father."

Tate wrinkled up his nose. "Don't talk about my father that way."

Colby laughed and scooped up another bite. "But whether we're talking about you or Tatum Senior, you have to admit Greg doesn't seem to have that mysterious thing both of you have."

"I can't help that I ooze charm and confidence. I get it from my mother."

"I'm sure you'd like to think that, but when it comes to business, you are your father's son. Now the artistic side of you...that's all Mama Jasmin."

"You might have a point. I can't believe my life has turned upside down in two weeks," Tate said. "For years, it's been you and my family. All my decisions and plans revolved around what was best for all of you. But now I have Eldon...and for the first time in my life, I'm having trouble making a decision."

"All's fair in love and war. Especially when you're at war with the Bixbys."

Tate snorted.

"Look over what I gave you. You seem to forget that I know you so well. There might be an option in there you like."

"I still can't believe you put a tracker in my leather jacket."

Colby honestly couldn't believe he'd done it either. "I was worried about you. I could tell you were keeping something from me, and you never do that. I'm still not sure why you thought you couldn't talk to me about taking some time away."

Tate sighed. "I knew I could talk to you. I guess I thought I needed to figure out some things for myself. And instead of finding answers, I found Eldon."

"Funny how things work out, isn't it?"

"If only you knew," Tate said with a laugh.

Carol approached their table with a pitcher in hand. Colby attempted a smile but was pretty sure it ended up more of a grimace. He really didn't know what had gotten into him. It was as if his arrival in Mistletoe Falls changed him somehow.

He shivered at the thought. Then again, the town had certainly done a number on Tate, so anything was possible. Colby laughed at the fanciful notion and managed a real smile for Carol as she refilled their glasses.

"Oh, now that's much better." Carol patted Colby's shoulder then glanced at his plate. Its almost empty state got him another pleased shoulder pat. "You look like you need some dessert. I'll whip you up something special."

"Aww, thanks Carol." Colby nearly melted in his chair. Then Tate had to ruin the moment the second she walked away by snorting at him. "What?"

"You're being so...nice. It's bizarre. You're so serious all the time, and now you're purring like a kitten at the sweet grandma who runs the diner."

"Yeah, well...." Colby had zero comebacks to the accusation because Tate was completely right.

"So, was the gingerbread room better than the killer nutcracker suite?" Tate asked.

"Don't even get me started. Linus is a menace to society."

"Now that's just silly talk," Carol said as she placed a giant slab of pecan pie in front of Colby. "Unless you're talking about his driving. The amount of mailboxes and trash cans that man managed to destroy...Behind the wheel, he's a menace. Otherwise, he's the biggest sweetheart in town."

Colby scooped up a hunk of pie with the provided spoon and shoved it into his mouth before he argued. He wanted to remain on Carol's good side, and they clearly had differing opinions where Linus was concerned.

After Colby and Tate devoured their dessert, Tate headed to his studio to take a look at the files Colby had prepared for him. Since they planned to meet again for dinner, Colby hoped something he'd worked on would give Tate some peace of mind.

As he approached the Inn, however, he realized peace of mind was one thing he'd never get as long as he was in Mistletoe Falls. A ridiculously tall ladder leaned against the front of the Inn, and to Colby's horror, Linus was on the roof without a safety line in sight.

The man was an absolute terror, but if something happened to him when Colby could have prevented it....

With a sigh, Colby climbed the ladder. When Linus paused from doing whatever it was he was doing, Colby cleared his throat. Luckily, he didn't scare Linus this time.

Instead, he turned to stare at Colby with a very cute. if confused. frown. "Why are you on the ladder? That's really not safe," Linus said.

Colby wanted to bang his head against the roof. "Yes, I know, which is why I came to find out why you were up here without a safety harness in sight."

"Oh, well, a bunch of my lights are out. I need to fix them before the light parade this weekend."

"And none of your cousins were available to assist? Isn't Oberon a handyman? Surely he has the appropriate equipment to climb around on a roof."

"Of course he does. Why wouldn't he? But since you're up here, you can help. Can you go flip the switch by the front door so I can see what's still out?"

"Not unless you sit down and don't move until I get back."

"You really are the strangest man," Linus said.

But he sat down, which drew Colby's attention to the sweater Linus wore. It was covered with red, white, blue, and green snowflakes. But it also had what appeared to be a faux blue tie with a jaunty snowman and matching faux suspenders.

Colby blinked at the dizzying pattern before shaking his head as he headed back down the ladder. Once inside, he flipped the switch conveniently labeled "roof lights" before going back out to see if he could help.

Linus glanced around the roof with a frown.

From where Colby stood, not a single light appeared to be out. "Looks like you fixed it."

"Yeah." Linus didn't seem convinced and continued eyeing the lights suspiciously.

"I'll hold the ladder. Come on down."

"You know I put all of these lights up by myself, right?"

"I did not know that, and I will be having a conversation with your cousins about it tonight at dinner."

"Ugh," Linus grunted when he reached the bottom. He turned and faced Colby, ending up inches away. "You're such a tattle tale."

"Am not."

"Are too."

"Am not."

Linus glared. "Are too, no take backs. Oh! Since you're so worried about ladder safety, you can help me get some mistletoe from the trees out back for the pyre. It doesn't look right yet. It needs some decoration or it just looks like a giant bonfire and not an alter."

"Alter?" Colby said. "I thought—"

"You should read up on Winter Solstice traditions before you judge, Colby."

"I wasn't judging!"

Linus pursed his lips and raised his brows.

"I wasn't." Colby quickly realized he wasn't going to win the argument. He sighed. "Fine, let's go get some mistletoe."

Linus removed the ladder with an expertise that shouldn't have shocked Colby. Within minutes, he had it folded down to an easy to carry size.

"That ladder is magic," Colby said. "How does it fold up like that?"

"Well, first, I say *abracadabra*," Linus said.

"Now who's judging?"

Linus carried the ladder around the back of the house with a laugh, then managed to get it unfolded and leaning against the same poor tree he'd tried to chop down. "I'll toss it down, so watch your face."

"I can't watch my own face. My eyes don't turn that way."

Linus smirked before looking him up and down. "Do you not own anything that isn't black? Honestly, Colby. There are other colors."

"Technically, black isn't a color."

"I'm going to *technically* you in a second. Hold the ladder so you don't fuss at me for being unsafe."

Colby watched Linus climb up the ladder, suddenly realizing that he enjoyed the view a little more than he should. He licked his lips and swallowed before forcing himself to look away. The ladder rattled a little, and he jerked his head up again to find Linus reaching for a green bundle tucked around a branch of the tree.

"Don't stretch so far!"

"Don't yell at me!"

Okay, Linus might have a point with that one. Colby leaned his weight against the ladder, determined not to let it slip as Linus continued to reach out to the surrounding branches, grabbing small bundles of the greenery and throwing them down.

"That should do it," Linus said, looking down at Colby. "Why are you so pale?"

There were several answers that came to mind as Linus began his descent, but Colby didn't care to share any of them. "Show me how the ladder works in case I have to save you from yourself at some point. It seems like I'm the only one who worries about your safety."

Linus shook his head. "Oh, my cousins worry, they've just given up arguing with me."

"I have gotten the sense that you're a bit stubborn."

"You know, you're beginning to remind me of Santa what with all this gracing me with your *presents* you keep doing."

Colby chuckled. "That was a good one. I approve. And just think, when I'm gone, you'll have all these *Santa*-mental memories to remember me by."

Linus groaned. "Stop making puns. You're cute when you're punny. I don't like it."

After elbowing Colby in the side, Linus showed him how to break down the ladder while explaining its multiple safety features and making sure Colby knew it was a gift from Oberon.

Colby gathered the mistletoe and carried it over to the pyre/alter/bonfire thing while Linus put the ladder back in the workshop under the carriage house. When Linus returned, he had some sheers and a spool of bright red ribbon in his hands.

Even though he really should get to his emails, Colby stayed and learned how to make mistletoe ornaments to decorate the pyre. He had to admit, the greenery and ribbon added a nice touch.

"It looks great," Colby said.

Linus stepped back and eyed his creation critically. Colby had watched Tate do the same thing to his own artwork. After a minute, Linus smiled and nodded. "It'll do."

"It'll more than do. Any Yule worshipers will be really grateful for all the hard work you've put into this, Linus. I'm sure it'll mean a lot to them."

Linus looked away, then waved his hand over his shoulder. "Go... work or something. You're getting me all emotional. I have things to accomplish. And no, they do not involve me climbing on ladders. Be gone!"

Colby did as he was told, heading to the little room they'd transformed into his office. All they'd really needed to do was carry down the desk, but Colby really appreciated it. He lost himself in his work for several hours, only stopping when his watch dinged a reminder that he needed to meet Tate and the others for dinner.

After glancing down at his all-black outfit, Colby made a trip upstairs to his room. Maybe had something Linus would approve of in his bag, even though he doubted it.

When he opened the door to his room, Colby pulled up short. For a second, he thought he'd opened the wrong door, but no, his iPad and charging station still sat on the nightstand where he left them.

Colby had no idea when Linus had found the time to redecorate his room, but all the gingerbread men and houses were gone. Instead, he had his own little cozy cocoa shoppe, complete with a cocoa making station on the dresser.

Linus had even given him a huge jar full of tiny little marshmallows and a coffee mug holder with Santa Claus mugs. It was one of the nicest things anyone had ever done for him. Colby glanced at his watch and realized he had enough time to make a mug before he needed to get downstairs to dinner.

And maybe he'd give Tate a quick call, too. Eldon might have some appropriate holiday wear in his shop that Colby could buy. The

least he could do was participate in the spirit of the season, especially since it seemed to mean so much to Linus and his family.

4

LINUS

His preparations were *almost* complete.

Linus rubbed his hands together with glee as he knelt in the bushes in the predawn hours of the morning. He only needed one more piece to make his Yule offering to the goddess, and he happened to know exactly where to find what he needed.

He tiptoed closer, moving the rope in his hand to form a little loop.

"Come here, little one. You're so sweet, aren't you? Like they need you for the nativity. Silly humans. Come on. I have some yummy treats for you."

Linus held out his gloved hand, and the baby goat he sought scurried closer, eager to eat the offering. Barely withholding a triumphant shout, Linus looped the rope around the goat's neck and led her out of the pen where the other animals were being housed.

It wasn't like anyone would miss one tiny, little baby goat. Besides, he was simply borrowing Matilda for the night. He'd return her once he'd finishing making his offering to the goddesses. His mission was more important than a nativity scene minus *one* baby goat for *one* night.

Linus and Matilda scampered through the woods to the Inn, where he immediately faced his first predicament. Where, exactly, could one keep a goat where it wouldn't be discovered, thereby ruining Linus's brilliant plan?

Then Linus remembered the metal puppy pen Oberon had bought for Jolly which she had immediately rejected, howling and protesting until Oberon gave in and abandoned the idea.

"Well, Matilda, looks like you and I have a fun day ahead of us."

Linus managed to get both the pen and Matilda upstairs to the cousins' shared living room. He spread out an old plastic tablecloth on the floor, put Matilda and nice bowl of fresh water in the pen, then sat down in his chair with his newest knitting project.

He put a video on television showing funny baby goat antics. Matilda didn't seem entertained, but Linus found it hysterically funny. She lay down and dozed while Linus waited until it was time to prepare breakfast for the Inn's guests.

Thanks to overnight shipping, Linus was also in possession of a brand new bag of goat feed. He'd thought this through with the precision of Santa planning his Christmas route. Nothing could go wrong.

"Linus?"

"Dag nab it!" Linus ran for the stairs, meeting Colby at the bottom with a beaming smile. "Hi, hello! Good morning!"

"Something's wrong with the internet." Colby held up his phone and waved it around. "I can't find a signal anywhere."

"Well, let's just go check on that, shall we?" Linus looped his arm through Colby's and practically dragged him away from the stairs.

"What's that noise?" Colby asked.

Matilda was not happy about being left alone. "Oh, ha ha! Just a kid. Um, on television." Technically, neither statement was a lie. Baby goats were called kids, and he also had them on the TV so...,

"Huh. But yeah, where's your router? I think it needs to be reset."

"Sure, sure. Routers. Um...where is that silly thing? Oh right! Utility room. Ha ha! Silly me."

Colby stopped moving. Since Linus still had a hold on him, it pulled him to a stop as well. "Linus...what are you up to?"

"Who me? Nothing special. You know. Same old, same old. Isn't it a beautiful day?"

"I don't know. I haven't been outside yet. Have you?"

"Have I? Have I? I bu...ju...bu...I wouldn't, um. Good morning!"

"Well, that wasn't suspicious at all."

"Utility room. Let's fix that router."

Linus tugged Colby's arm and led him to the little closet where all the electronics were stored. The router's lights blinked the way they usually did, at least as far as Linus could see.

"Look! A router." Linus beamed and gestured to the black box.

"I see. Mind if I reset it?"

"Mind? Why no. I wouldn't mind. You just do that while I...go... make breakfast. Right. That's what I'm going to do. See you!"

Linus darted back upstairs and found Matilda out of the pen, chewing on a limb of the Christmas tree. "Matilda! Don't eat the tree. Here. I'll get you some yummy breakfast and then we'll go for walksies so you can potty...which I see you already did. On the rug."

Matilda bleated at him, her snowy white coat absolutely adorable against the backdrop of the tree.

Linus whipped out his phone and snapped a pic. "You're so cute. Sweet little girl. Now let's get back in the pen and not be an escape artist for Uncle Linus, okay?"

After cleaning up the wee little mess Matilda made, Linus scurried back downstairs. He found Colby waiting at the kitchen table, tapping away on his phone.

"Router fixed?" Linus asked cheerily.

"Yep. You gonna tell me what you're doing yet?"

"Fixing breakfast! Are you hungry? None of our guests are breakfasting in this morning. Several of them got an early start."

"So...you've been up for a while. I guess that explains it."

"Explains what?"

"Why you're acting...off."

"Ha ha! I'm not off. I'm on! Fire. On fire. Wait, no. No fires. Um. Breakfast. Hey, do you know what Santa's second favorite snack is?"

Colby blinked at him.

"Kringle cut fries! Get it? *Kringle* cut."

"I got it," Colby said.

"Okay, here's some delicious oatmeal for that big lawyer brain of yours. Good energy for the mind. You'll get lots done today."

"I know you're going to do something I'm really not going to like, and yet I realize there's little to nothing I can do to stop you. Besides, I have a feeling part of your sleep deficit is because you snuck around yesterday redecorating my room. I really appre—"

"I what now?"

"My room? The whole cocoa thing."

Linus blinked, then blinked again. "Excuse me for a moment."

He took off running for the stairs and dashed down the hall to Colby's room. He flung open the door and found it completely redone...and not by him. "Huh."

"Linus? Is something wrong?"

"Nope! It's perfect. I thought I forgot something, but nope! Sure didn't. But boy am I tired from all that hard work and getting up so early. I think I'm going to head upstairs and take a nap. Yep. So, you do your brain work and I'll be...napping."

Colby had his bowl of oatmeal in his hands, so Linus ushered him into the parlor-turned-office and shut the door. Then he ran back to the upstairs living room.

Matilda was seconds away from chewing on his favorite holiday pillow. He'd cross-stitched it himself. He pulled it away from her teeth and scooped her up into his arms. "Now listen, you've gotta be really quiet."

She bleated her agreement.

Linus grabbed the rope he'd used as a leash earlier and carried her downstairs. They snuck out of the back door before Linus put her down and allowed her to chew on some grass and do her business. He really should have done a little bit more research on goats before enacting his plan.

He couldn't help it though. What were the odds the local nativity would decide to add a petting zoo to their stable the exact year he needed a Yule goat for the pyre? Slim to none.

Linus could read a sign as well as the next sprite. Matilda was meant to be. Now he just had to hide her until dusk when he could do the whole goat-pyre ritual and beg forgiveness so he could get his very own mate.

Matilda bleated, and Linus took it to mean she'd finished her morning constitutional. He'd really have to clean that up later. How could something so little make such a big...mess?

After sneaking Matilda back upstairs, Linus made her several decorative bows to wear during the ritual, then went back to his knitting. He actually lost track of time until Matilda bleated once more, and he realized she'd not only eaten the magazine on the table, but she'd made another mess on the floor.

He cleaned up once more, lectured her on the importance of not eating things she wasn't supposed to, then dressed her in her bows and ribbons. She looked absolutely precious.

With his sturdy candle lighter tucked safely in his pocket, Linus snuck down the stairs. He made sure the coast was clear, then stealthily made his way out of the back door. He put Matilda down while he unplugged the silly electric log—honestly, Linus couldn't believe Colby had fallen for that one—then knelt by the pyre to light the kindling.

"Ah ha!"

"Ahhhhh!" Linus screamed and grabbed Matilda, holding her protectively against him.

"I knew you were up to something. You told me you weren't going to light the pyre, Linus. It's not even Winter Solstice yet."

"How do you know that?"

"Because I looked it up. You're right, I should know—hey, don't distract me. And why are you holding a baby goat? Oh my god, are you going to sacrifice the goat on the pyre? No. Absolutely not. Give me the goat, Linus."

"Sacrifice...Colby! You think I'm a goat murderer? Is that what you really think of me? How...how...why...how...You're a horrible person! I don't like you at all!"

Colby glared and stomped toward him. "Give me the goat, Linus."

"No! I'm not a goat murderer you...you...grinch face!" Linus turned away from Colby only to feel Colby's hand in his back pocket.

"Ah ha! Proof. You were going to light the fire and sacrifice that sweet little baby goat."

"I most certainly was not. You heathen! Clearly you didn't read anything about Winter Solstice rituals. or you would know that goats are honored not murdered. Horrible excuse for a human being. I don't even know why Tate is friends with you. So suspicious of everyone. You're awful. He's awful, isn't he Matilda?

Matilda bleated her agreement.

"See? Even Matilda thinks you're awful."

Colby shook the lighter in his hand. "You were going to light it. Don't deny it."

"I thought we should have a practice round. To make sure it worked."

Colby's eye began to twitch again. He really should have that looked at.

"We agreed it was not going to be lit. That it was too close to the Inn and other homes. That there were permits and other permissions needed."

"I did forget the permits part," Linus confessed. "But I have a fire extinguisher. It'll be fine. Just...you know, give me back the lighter."

"I don't think so."

"Dag nab it!" Linus stomped his foot. "You're ruining everything."

Matilda bleated.

"If you say that Matilda agrees with you, I will take her right now. I happen to know the way to a very nice tree farm where I'm sure she would live a long and happy life."

Linus gasped. "You would never."

"Try me."

"Fine! Matilda and I are going back upstairs. You can get your own dinner because I'm not making you anything. So there!"

"Fine. I'll dig around in your kitchen, then. I'm sure I can come up with something. I won't make too big of a mess, either."

"You evil, evil man."

"Gimme the goat and let's go inside."

Linus narrowed his eyes. "You aren't keeping her."

"I'm not keeping her."

"Swear you'll give her back to me."

"I will, as long as you swear that you will absolutely not under any circumstances light that pyre."

"It seems we have reached an impasse." Linus tapped his foot on the ground. Matilda wiggled in his arms, so he sat her down and she immediately peed. "What a good girl. Good potty, Matilda!"

When he looked back at Colby, not only was his eye twitching, but a vein bulged in his forehead.

Linus reached up and poked it. "We should probably get that looked at," Linus said gently. "You could be having a seizure or something."

"I'm not having a seizure. I'm having Linus-itus. It's probably contagious because everyone around here seems to think you're sweet and innocent."

"So you're not having a seizure?" Linus asked. "Because your eye is twitch—"

"I'm not having a seizure, Linus! Don't light the pyre, okay?"

"Fine. Sheesh. All you had to do was ask. You really should work on your temper. Matilda is scared."

Linus scooped Matilda up and carried her into the kitchen. He fixed her a bowl of goat feed before washing his hands and trying to figure out what to make for dinner.

"I need a drink," Colby said.

"I have some lovely scotch in the living room. Help yourself." Linus smiled pleasantly until Colby waved the lighter and carried it out of the room with him.

He was back a second later. "Linus."

"Colby, I already said I wouldn't light the pyre. Let it go."

"Someone punked you," Colby said. "I'm...I don't know...you should come see this."

Considering the twitching and throbbing going on with Colby's face, Linus figured it was serious. He followed him into the lobby... and found it decked out in shamrocks. Everything was green and gold. Not a Christmas decoration in sight.

Linus whimpered. "My pretties."

"It's okay. We can fix it. Do you have security cameras? If I find out who did this to you—"

Linus turned to Colby and couldn't resist flinging his arms around his waist. "Forget everything I said earlier. You're the sweetest man. Now, let's eat dinner and take care of Matilda. It's her first night in her new home, so I want to make sure she feels safe and secure."

Colby took the hand Linus held out and they went back into the kitchen. Matilda had found the mat by the kitchen sink and chewed on it. After fussing at her once more, Linus made them a nice pasta with a lemon and Parmesan sauce.

"I really don't understand anything about my life right now," Colby said as they washed up the few dishes.

Colby carried Matilda upstairs for Linus since he had his hands full with some extra hay left over from his Samhain decorations.

Hopefully, she'd find it much tastier to munch on than any of his belongings.

"Don't worry. I've been stocking up on some yummy treats. We can watch a movie. Hey, do you know who Santa's favorite cartoon character is?"

"I'm afraid to ask," Colby said as he put Matilda in the pen.

"Chimney Cricket. Get it? *Chimney*?"

"I get it, Linus. I definitely get it."

5

COLBY

"Morning, sunshine," Tate said when Colby answered his phone the following morning.

He took a sip of the cocoa he'd made for himself in his room before replying. "It *is* a good morning."

"Who are you and what have you done with my best friend?"

Colby laughed and finished typing the email he'd been composing when the phone rang. After hitting send, Colby grabbed his cocoa mug again. "I'm the guy who has a mug of marshmallows with a little cocoa on top."

"So you're on a sugar high. Check. I went through all the paperwork you prepped for me. I'd like to talk it over with you. Would you mind coming to the studio?"

"No problem. I'll be there in a few."

A knock on his office door drew his attention next. "Come in."

"Morning," Linus said, balancing both a tray and Matilda's leash in one hand. "We brought you a snack and a little present."

"A present?" Colby leaned over to scratch Matilda's head, earning himself a soft little bleat of happiness from her.

Linus sat down the tray which had a flaky chocolate croissant on it before producing a gift bag from behind his back. "It's...if you hate it, it's okay."

Colby took the bag and pulled out the decorative tissue paper. Inside, Colby saw a blur of bright colors. He pulled the bundle out and found a rainbow striped sweater.

"I know. It's a lot," Linus said. "I shouldn't have made it. I had all these pieces of yarn left and I don't know, it turned into a sweater. You don't—"

"I love it," Colby said.

He stood and pulled on the sweater over the black turtleneck he wore. It fit perfectly.

"Really?" Linus asked.

"Really. It's so soft. How'd you make it so soft? It's like I'm wearing a hug."

Linus laughed. "It's the yarn, silly man. I thought you might like to wear it to the town's light parade tonight. You know, fit in with the festivities and all."

"You don't think I'm taking it off again, do you? I'll be wearing it all day, thank you very much."

Linus beamed. "I'm glad you like it. Matilda kept me up a lot last night, so I had extra time to finish it."

"Well, I have to go meet Tate, but when I get back, I'll goat-sit so you can take a nap. We don't need a tired Linus on light parade night, now do we?"

Linus beamed and shook his head. "Okay, get back to work. We'll see you later."

"Don't start any fires."

"I won't. Sheesh. Can you believe him, Matilda? A guy wants to light a pyre one time and he never hears the end of it."

Colby laughed and turned back to his laptop, shooting off another email that couldn't wait before snagging his mug of cocoa for the walk over to Tate's studio.

During the night, Linus had managed to redecorate the lobby to its former glory, removing all traces of the Saint Patrick's Day shenanigans. It was no wonder the poor guy looked about ready to collapse. How he managed to get so much decorating done on top of his other tasks was really astounding.

The difference in the past few days in Mistletoe Falls also surprised Colby. Although he'd seen some tourists during the week, the town square bustled with shoppers even though it wasn't even noon on Friday. Maybe the town's light parade was a bigger deal than Colby realized. He'd certainly heard enough about it to make him think so.

Although the Snowda Shoppe, the business that came along with the building Tate bought, remained closed, Colby had a key. He went inside, marveled at the over-the-top decor Eldon had managed for a business that wasn't even open for the holiday season, then made his way up to the second floor where Tate had his studio set up.

He expected to find Tate in front of his easel, painting away in the morning light. Instead, Tate had a standing desk set up with a treadmill beneath it. He walked as he studied the monitor in front of him, dictating notes into his phone as he did.

Colby knocked on the door to get Tate's attention. He ended the recording session before hopping off the treadmill. "You made it."

"I told you I was on my way."

"True, but in this town, you never know what'll come up between the Tinseled Inn and the town square. It's two blocks of chaos and confusion."

Colby laughed. "I think you've had a bit too much eggnog my friend. The only chaos in Mistletoe Falls is back at the Inn, and his name is Linus."

Tate grabbed a printed stack of paperwork from the desk and turned to him once more. Then he froze, his eyes wide. "What... are...you...wearing?"

"A sweater. Linus knitted it for me."

"Sweet Santa in a sleigh, you've become one of them."

"Says the man wearing a Snowda Shoppe T-shirt when said shop isn't even open."

"Hey! I found these in the loft. I needed some workout gear."

"Uh-huh. And did a certain cute guy who works next door have a hand in designing said T-shirts."

Tate scowled. "Maybe. Shut up. Now get over here and go through this stuff with me. I can't decide if you're a genius or a monster. Or whose side you're on. It's very confusing, and I'm used to that wicked brain of yours."

Colby took a sip of cocoa, making sure to get a nice bunch of marshmallows in the process as he sat down on the couch. Tate clearly had a case of the nerves after having seen all his options laid out in black and white. They'd been through this process many times over the years, so Colby sat back and waited. Besides, who wanted cold cocoa? Not him. He'd have plenty of time to drink while Tate fumed.

As predicted, Tate grabbed the stacked pages and pulled the first few off the top. "This is a big fat no. I'm not going back to my old life, one hundred percent. Nice try with this one, asshole. I have Eldon to think about now, and you know it."

Colby nodded as Tate ripped the suggestion in half and tossed it aside.

"And same with this one. How exactly do you think I could live in Mistletoe Falls full time? I have responsibilities, and if you think I'm going to just walk away from my family, you don't know me at all."

Colby held back his snort. Of course he knew Tate. Which was why he'd put the worst two options first.

Now they had to get to the tricky bits. Tate had to decide how he wanted to spend his time, and Colby couldn't make that decision for him. All he could do was lay out the options and let his best friend figure it out.

He took another big gulp of cocoa and marshmallows while he waited.

"Now this has some merit," Tate said, eyeing option three. "Splitting my time fifty-fifty seems fair. It gives me time to paint, time with Eldon, but time with the family and business as well."

Of course, the option seemed fair, but Colby knew it wasn't what Tate wanted. He'd figure it out.

"I'd be doing more remote work with this option, which would allow me additional time in Mistletoe Falls. We'd have to figure out a better living situation, though. The Inn is lovely, but I'm not sure I—"

"Turn to Appendix E," Colby said

Tate frowned and grabbed the stack. He flipped pages until he reached the appendixes. "You picked out houses for me."

"Well, no. I found a few properties which could be viable, depending on what you choose to do. There are homes available here that should suit your needs."

Tate side-eyed him. "You know me too well. It's creepy."

"I think the fourth property is the one you'll like best, but I could be wrong."

"You're never wrong, so stop being smug while I look at house number four. Ass."

House four happened to be located two doors down from the Tinseled Inn. Technically, it wasn't on the market yet, but a quick call to the real estate office in town yielded him the extra information that the family living there planned on selling in the spring.

Which, if Colby's calculations were correct—and they were—would be about the time Tate and Eldon would be able to focus on moving in to a new home. Plus, with early knowledge of the place in mind, Eldon would be able to do his decorating thing and get everything ordered in advance. Home decor at the level Eldon and Tate would require meant ordering pieces months in advance.

"Okay, stop distracting me with real estate. I haven't even made a decision yet."

"I know," Colby said.

"Now, option four and five are lumped together. Two-thirds of my time one way or the other. I see your strategy here. It allows for flexibility depending on what's going on with the businesses. We could still buy a house here, but I could keep my apartment in town when I'm needed at corporate. Hmm."

Colby waited. Tate's eyes moved back and forth over the three remaining options. He waited. And waited.

"Say something," Tate yelled. "You're being all smug and know-it-all again."

"Appendix B."

"What's in Appendix B?"

"Something you didn't bother reading because you never read the appendixes even though I spend quite a bit of time gathering additional information for you."

Tate growled under his breath but flipped to the back again.

"No. Absolutely not."

Colby took his final gulp of cocoa and chewing the mushy deliciousness of melted marshmallows. Victory was so, so sweet."

"I am not inviting my family here for Christmas to meet Eldon and talk this all through. No way. Are you kidding me? I need to...."

"What's that?" Colby asked. "You need to...maybe talk this over with your new boyfriend and let him meet your family. Oh, and maybe tell your family what your life's dream is so maybe they can be part of it instead of treating your talent like some dirty secret that needs to be hidden away? Now there's a thought."

"Asshole."

"Tatum William Bixby the third!" Eldon stood in the doorway with his arms crossed over his chest. "Don't talk to your best friend that way. Also, Colby, you have a cocoa mustache. Not cute. And, um, that sweater...."

"Linus knitted it for him," Tate explained.

"Oh. He did? Huh. That explains it. Never mind. Now why are you calling Colby names?"

"Because he's being all logical and I don't like it."

"Appendix B," Colby said, pointing to the papers in Tate's hand.

Eldon grabbed the stack, read the appendix, then turned to Tate. "This one. Make it happen."

"You didn't even read the other options," Tate said.

"Why would I? This is the right answer and we both know it. From the smug look on Colby's face, he knows it as well. So, get on the phone, sweet talk your mom, and get them all here next week. Friday should work. I'll let Linus know. We normally don't have guests from the solstice on, although I know Linus made one exception for a couple who wanted to stay on the solstice. They're only in for a couple nights, though, and then the Inn is free. Well, except for Colby, of course."

Tate looked back and forth between them before throwing his hands in the air. "Fine, I'll call my mother."

"Oh," Eldon said. "I didn't know the Peterson's were moving in the spring. It makes sense, though. Their daughter is a nurse and can't really get away during the holidays. They've been wanting to spend more time with their grandkids. It's a gorgeous house."

"My work here is done."

"Au contraire," Eldon said. "We have a town emergency. All hands on deck."

"What's going on?" Tate asked.

"We have a missing goat from the church's nativity petting zoo. We're putting together a search and rescue missing. Poor thing must have gotten out of the pen and is roaming around somewhere."

"A goat?" Colby said.

"Don't judge, Colby. She's a sweet little baby goat and she needs our help."

Colby nodded. "No doubt."

"So we can count on your help?"

"Looking for the goat? Sure. I'll help. No problem."

"We're printing flyers, too. Here. Take a few and hang them up on the lampposts on your way to the inn. You'll want some different shoes, I'm sure."

Colby didn't need to worry about his shoes. He stared down at the papers in his hand and tried not to react. The flyers had a color photo of Matilda with the words *Have You Seen This Goat?* printed beneath. It even had little tear tabs with a phone number to call.

"Right. I'm going to go change my shoes. I'll see you later, Tate. Say hi to your mom for me."

Colby hurried back to the Tinseled Inn, not sure if he wanted to strangle Linus or...well, he didn't know what else he wanted to do to the man. He could outline Tate's future in an evening while adding appendixes and babysitting a goat, but understanding why he was having such strange reactions to a quirky Inn owner?

Baffled was the best word to describe his feelings on the matter.

When he didn't find Linus inside, he looked out the back window, and sure enough, he found Linus marching around the pyre—unlit or he'd have had to raise his voice to Linus and he really didn't want to do that—with a red-ribboned Matilda at his side.

"I didn't light it," Linus said the moment he caught sight of Colby.

"You are a dirty goat-napper."

Linus gasped. "What? First I'm a murderer and now I'm a—"

Colby held the flyer up in front of Linus's face.

"—dirty goat-napper," Linus said. "Dag nab it."

"I cannot believe you stole a goat from the church nativity, Linus. What were you thinking?"

"I didn't steal her! I borrowed Matilda. Borrowed, Colby. There's a big difference and you should know better."

"Did you ask permission to borrow Matilda? Did you tell anyone where she was? Or give them a time when you planned on returning her?"

"Well, no."

"So you goat-napped her."

Linus's face fell. "It was really important, Colby. I know you don't understand, but will you at least believe me when I tell you I did it for a really good reason? And no, I can't explain it."

Considering Linus suddenly looked like he was about to burst into tears, Colby pulled him into a hug and patted his back. "I know you were trying to make Winter Solstice special. My guess is that the special guests coming in that night are...what? Pagan? Wiccan? And you were trying to make them feel accepted."

Linus didn't look up. He didn't move. At all.

"Linus?"

"You're going to take her back, aren't you?"

"Yes, Linus. I'm going to take her back. She doesn't belong to you."

"But we've bonded, Colby. I even knitted her a sweater to match yours."

Colby sighed. "I'm taking her back to the petting zoo, Linus. And then you and I are having a long talk."

6

LINUS

L inus skulked behind Colby as he led Matilda down the sidewalk. He ducked behind a tree when Colby turned to look behind him. After a second, Colby continued down the sidewalk.

Linus crept out from behind the tree and hurried to a large bush in the neighbor's yard. He leapt behind it when Colby turned around again.

"Linus, I can see you. Just get up here and walk with me."

Dag nab it. He'd been hoping he could pull off another goat-napping—*ahem*—goat *borrowing*. Although he hadn't been able to come up with a plan that would get both him and Matilda away from Colby, especially when Colby would just go back to the Inn and find them. As far as plans went, it needed some serious work.

Linus attempted another tactic. "But Colby, we don't *have* to take her back. I love her! Look at how happy she is with us."

Colby's look didn't make Linus hopeful. "This is what's known as a teachable moment, Linus. She doesn't belong to you, so we're taking her back."

"*Teachable moment. Meh meh meh.*"

"I can hear you." Colby didn't bother stopping as Linus stomped along beside him.

Matilda bleated.

"I know, Matilda," Linus said forlornly. "He's so mean. He didn't even compliment you on your jingle bell harness *or* your sweater."

Colby's sigh shook the branches of the evergreen tree on the corner.

"He's so dramatic," Linus whispered to Matilda. "I thought lawyers were supposed to be serious."

She bleated her agreement.

Colby stopped and turned to face him. "Linus, Matilda looks gorgeous in her sweater. I love that she's jingling all the way back to the nativity where she belongs looking so beautiful. There. Is that good enough for you?"

"Well, I wouldn't say it's a *glowing* review, but I suppose we'll take it, right Matilda?"

Matilda took the chance to snack on one of the lowest tree branches since they weren't moving. She didn't really seem impressed by Colby's praise, though. "So much for lawyers making convincing arguments. When you can't even convince a goat...."

The weird vein on Colby's forehead popped out again. Linus made a mental note to talk to Miles about it. It was certainly worrying Linus every time it appeared. It would be nice to talk to the new doctor in the family to make sure it wasn't anything serious.

"Come along, Matilda," Colby said.

He gave her leash a gentle tug, encouraging her to follow him. She jingled along beside him down the sidewalk toward town square, not realizing Colby was ruining their plans for the perfect pyre.

Linus huffed and hurried to catch up. Their appearance drew a lot of attention as they approached the circle in the center of town. Linus waved at everyone who stared. They smiled and waved back.

"I think they're admiring your sweater," Linus said. "It really is cheerful. Look at all the smiles you're getting."

"Or it could be that the goat I'm walking on a reindeer-worthy jingle bell leash through downtown Mistletoe Falls has a matching sweater to mine. I mean, I could be wrong, but that certainly seems like something that would draw this many stares."

"Well, now that you brought it up, the two of you are incredibly sweet together. You know if we just take her back...is your eye twitching *again*, Colby? That's it. I'm calling Miles."

"Don't call the vet, Linus. I don't need a vet."

"You know, maybe we should take Matilda to—"

"We're taking her back to her owners, Linus. Stop trying to get me to change my mind. You broke the law. We're taking her back to the nativity where she belongs."

Linus huffed. "You've made that abundantly clear. Sheesh. You really like the sound of your own voice, don't you? You're always repeating yourself."

Colby's eye really began twitching a lot. Luckily, they'd almost reached the church. Linus would make sure they took the path nearest Paws and Claus when they went home so Miles could check Colby over.

As they approached the nativity, a lady dressed all in white stood by the pen. She caught sight of them and froze. Instead of the beaming smile Linus expected over the triumphant return of Matilda, she frowned. How could anyone frown at someone as incredibly cute as Matilda? Someone evil, that's who.

"I knew it," Linus grumbled.

"Matilda!" The lady hurried toward them, stopping them before they could get too close to the other animals.

"We found your missing goat," Colby said with the brightest, fakest smile Linus had ever seen. He scowled and tried to kick Colby's ankle, but he slipped and nearly fell. Colby caught him without his smile fading in the slightest.

Linus huffed at him. "*So disappointed. Won't even let me keep my goat.*"

Mean lady looked back and forth between them with a puzzled frown. "Isn't that...nice."

Linus couldn't take it anymore. "You...you...aren't nice! You don't love Matilda. Colby, she doesn't love Matilda!"

Colby closed his eyes and looked up to the sky. Probably checking in with the goddess. Linus did the same thing on occasion, but normally in private. To each their own though. Who was he to say how someone else communed with their deity?

"Should I put her in the pen for you?" Colby asked.

"Uh...well...."

"See!"

"Linus, you aren't helping," Colby said.

"I'm helping Matilda! She's the one I care about."

Colby gave him a rather stern look before returning his attention to the really not nice lady. Honestly, who wore an angel outfit near so many animals? Matilda had already plucked one of the feathers off of her wings. She was such a good goat.

"You know, Matilda doesn't really get along with the other animals. We brought in Petunia to take her place during the nativity after Matilda tried to eat the hay out of the manger. Let's just say it was a very close call with the baby Jesus."

"So... you don't want her," Linus said. He shot a triumphant stare Colby's way. "I mean, we would be happy to—"

"Linus."

"—keep her. She would be *so* happy with us. We would give her a great home."

"You'd do that for her?" The lady wasn't really all that awful now that Linus thought about it. And her outfit was pretty, except for the missing feathers. She probably should fix that. It really threw off the entire ensemble.

"We would," Linus said. "A thousand million percent would. We love her already!"

Colby lowered his head onto his hand and muttered under his breath. He was clearly overwrought, the sweet man. Matilda could do that to a guy. All that cuteness in one tiny, little bleating package. Who could resist?

Linus patted him on the back. "It's okay, Colby. We can keep her. All's well that ends well."

"This was supposed to be a teachable moment," Colby grumbled.

"Lesson learned," Linus said. "I was right, and you were wrong. Now, let's get Matilda home. I saw this really cute goat play set online and want to see if I can have it here by Christmas. She'd be so cute playing on it. Oh, and we can build a little fence around it so she can run around and have fun without being on a leash. I'd let her loose in the backyard, but I'm worried about my roses. What if she gets cut by a thorn? But we can make her a special area that's just for her, can't we, Colby? This is *so* exciting."

"I don't know where I went wrong," Colby said. "It seemed so straightforward, then *wham*, it all went awry. Is it something in the water? Is this town cursed? Am I being pranked? Is it Opposite Day?"

"Maybe you should eat," Linus said. "Talking to yourself isn't a good sign. Probably low blood sugar. I'm sure Carol wouldn't mind if we stopped by for some takeout. I bet she'd love to meet Matilda."

Colby paused and looked over at Linus. "It's *too much* sugar. That has to bit it. All that cocoa I've been drinking. I should cut back."

"So, no dessert from Carol. Got it."

They walked down the block from the church to the corner where Carol's and Crepes was located. Colby still looked kinda stunned, although Linus wasn't sure why. They'd saved Matilda. What was there to be so surprised about?

"Why don't you sit here on the bench with Matilda while I go in and order?"

Linus guided Colby to a bench outside the diner, then patted his shoulder. He went inside to place an order with Carol, which she was sweet enough to offer to have someone deliver since Colby wasn't feeling well, then went back outside.

Several tourists surrounded Colby. Matilda had climbed up onto his lap and curled up into a little sleepy ball. Linus's heart melted. After letting them gush over Colby and Matilda's cuteness for another minute, Linus intervened.

Colby had never looked so happy to see him. It was a nice change from the typical scowls. And hey, the vein had gone away. That had to be a good sign.

"Let's go home," Linus said.

He held out his hand and Colby took it, adjusting the still sleeping Matilda so she was cradled in his arm. They made it all the way to their block before Colby had to go and ruin everything. He suddenly stopped and turned to Linus.

"I'm not taking one more step until you answer some questions." Colby planted his feet and adjusted Matilda so she was more secure in his arms.

"Are you sure? We could talk in the nice warm Inn. Doesn't that sound nice?"

"Linus, what are you planning on doing with the pyre? And be honest with me this time or I swear, I'll find a nice, lovely farm for Matilda to live. And I won't tell you where it is."

Linus's mouth fell open. "You wouldn't."

"I so would. Now talk."

Linus flopped dramatically into the neighbor's yard. "It's symbolic of my love life, Colby. There. That's the truth. *Now* do you feel better?"

"Your love...No, Linus. I don't feel better. That makes no sense at all."

"Oh, it doesn't make sense, does it? Well, what if all *your* cousins found their boyfriends within weeks and you were stuck being single *forever*? What if all you ever wanted was *your* special someone and everyone around you got someone, but *you* didn't? Huh? How about that? So, I'm going to light a pyre to symbolize the burning fire of regret and loss that is my love life. I'm letting go of the old, spiteful, bitter, jealous, and lonely Linus to make room for the new Linus who gets his own happily ever after."

Linus sucked in a deep breath from his position on the grass and stared up at Colby. He half-expected Colby to laugh at him, but instead, Colby kinda looked like he'd been shocked by a string of Christmas lights. Linus had done it himself one too many times to not recognize the expression.

"Um, Colby? You okay up there?" Linus didn't see any Christmas lights near them, but those sneaky little wires were sometimes hidden from view. Linus knew that from experience too.

Colby sank down onto the grass beside him. He put Matilda between them and let her roam while holding on to her leash. She began to nibble on the grass, her little harness jingling as she chewed.

"I think I just had a teachable moment," Colby mumbled.

"Oh. Is that good? Because mine turned out great."

Colby turned to glare at him. "Stealing is wrong, Linus. No more stealing."

"Borrowing, Colby. *Borrowing*. There's a big difference."

"Not according to the law."

"Well, I'm not talking to the law. I'm talking to you about Matilda. You're confounding sometimes."

"I'm...I'm..." Colby sputtered but didn't finish his thought. Then he dropped back onto the grass and laughed. Matilda climbed up on his chest and lay down.

Linus whipped out his phone, snapped a pic, then texted it to all his cousins. Honestly, there wasn't a cuter goat on the planet. And Colby was pretty cute too, now that he thought about it. Linus snapped another pic, this one of Colby's laughing face. He saved that one for himself.

"Colby?" Linus asked when Colby still hadn't moved or spoken in the time it took him to add a filter on the picture of Colby and Matilda and post it to the Inn's social media accounts.

"So, you burn the dead wood to make room for new growth." Colby whispered. His hand came up to gently pet Matilda's head.

"Oh, we're back to the pyre. Okay. Yes, we have to burn away the dead stuff in our life to make room for new growth. Lose the negative to add the positive. I shouldn't be jealous of my cousins," Linus confessed. "But I am. It's probably why the go...um, well, it's probably why I haven't found my own true love yet."

Colby rolled his head to the side and smiled at Linus. "I think you're really lovable. And cute, too."

Linus smiled back. "Yeah?"

He shivered a little at the intense look in Colby's eyes.

"Absolutely. Tell me more about the pyre."

"First off, you don't sacrifice goats on it, I can promise you that much. I still can't believe you thought I would murder Matilda. That's horrifying. What did you do? Look it up on Wikipedia?"

"Maybe? I didn't know where else to look for information on mysterious pyres and goats." Colby said. "So tell me more about what it actually means. It's clearly important to you. You know way too much about it for the pyre to just be for some random guests coming to visit."

"It's true," Linus said.

He lay back in the grass beside Colby and grinned when Colby reached for his hand. He wasn't even sure why the gesture warmed his heart and sent another little shiver down his spine.

Linus swallowed hard before beginning his explanation. "Winter is the darkest time of year. I mean, think about it. It gets dark so early and way back in the old days, that had to be a little scary, right? It wasn't like they had a nice warm Inn to call home. So, it's dark for more hours than it's light, and who knows what lurks out there in the darkness. But there's a reason for every season. The darkness doesn't have to be bad. We all need time to rest and recover. Time to think and reflect. When better than to do that than when you aren't out in the sunshine doing all the hard work?"

"That doesn't sound so bad. Slowing down would be nice."

"Exactly. Which is weird, because it's our busiest time of year in Mistletoe Falls, but my cousins and I...well, we believe in bringing light to the darkest times of year. I suppose you could say it's the way we were raised."

"And the pyre brings light?"

"Well, technically. But there are other ways to bring light. The pyre is just...I wanted to let go of those bad feelings to make room for new ones. That's all. It was really something I was doing for me. I don't like feeling negative, especially at this time of year, you know?"

Colby gave his hand a gentle squeeze. "I bet it has been hard for you. Does the pyre have to be on the solstice for it to work?"

"No. We do other things on the actual solstice as a family. Like I said, this was something for me to help me."

"Would it..." Colby paused and turned to look at him. "Can I do it too? I think I have a few things to let go of and make room for as well."

Linus turned away from the intense, emotional look in Colby's eyes. He stared up at the sky and wondered what had come over Colby. He certainly wasn't acting like himself. And, come to think of it, neither was Linus. "Yes, Colby. You can do it too."

"Thanks, Linus. That means a lot to me."

"No problem."

Their sentimental moment was broken by a loud voice yelling, "Are you two okay?"

Linus sat up and saw Miles standing on his front porch looking at them like they might be injured or something. "We're fine."

Miles didn't seem convinced. "Do I want to know why you're lying on the neighbor's lawn?"

"Probably not. But we're going now. Oh, and don't worry if you see smoke later."

Miles's eyes widened. "Linus."

"It's fine! Colby's watching out for me. Get back to work. Lots of puppies and kitties to take care of. I'll be making an appointment for Matilda next week."

Miles rubbed his hand over his hair.

Linus didn't know why he looked so confused.

"Matilda?"

"My new goat," Linus explained. "She's really sweet."

"Goat...."

Colby sat up and put Matilda on her feet. "We have a baby goat. The petting zoo didn't want her."

"Isn't that the missing goat from the nativity? Everyone in town has been searching for her."

"We found her," Linus said. "And then they didn't want her back. Horrible people, Miles. You should check on the rest of their animals. That woman said Matilda was naughty!"

"Well, she is trying to eat Colby's sweater."

Colby pulled her away from the hem of his sweater and stood. "See you later, Miles."

Linus climbed to his feet and reached for Colby's hand again. He didn't know why he did it, but Colby didn't seem to mind. They walked the rest of the way to the Inn without talking.

"So...we're really going to light it?" Linus asked when they reached the front door.

"We are. After we take about two-thirds of the wood off. We don't want to burn everything down, Linus. And I think there are some concrete blocks in the tool shop we can put around it to make a stone circle of sorts."

"I knew I should have gone with the star and not the log cabin."

"Well, if you'd told me this sooner, maybe we could have saved ourselves a lot of work."

Maybe.

But Linus had a sneaking suspicion the truth had come out exactly when it was supposed to. And wasn't that something interesting to think about.

7

COLBY

Much to Linus's horror, Colby insisted they chain Matilda to a tree on the opposite side of the backyard from the pyre. Colby tried both logic and reason to explain his demand. He didn't want her to get hurt by getting too close to the flames, and he didn't want her to be unattended inside. The safest bet was to keep her outside with them while they worked to get the pyre set to rights.

Linus wasn't having any of it.

In the end, Colby resorted to pouting. No logical argument would sway Linus. A pout? Well, it worked like magic.

"Oh you sweet man," Linus cooed. "You don't want to be without her. Well, all you had to do was say so. Let's get her set up on a nice patch of grass. then we'll get to work on the pyre."

Colby patted himself on the back—metaphorically, of course—as he followed Linus into the workshop. They found what they needed in the form of a long chain attached to a stake that could be planted into the ground.

"Obie probably bought it for Jingle," Linus explained as he removed the packaging. "But he doesn't let her out of his sight. I swear, it's like he's afraid to be without her for a second."

Colby had to bite his lip as Linus cooed at Matilda, promising the little goat that he wouldn't leave her sight. Once they had her settled, Colby and Linus carried out a stack of landscaping blocks and built a circle around the pyre. They took a quick break to eat the lunch delivered by one of Carol's staff members, then began the long task of reducing the towering pyre to a more reasonable level.

And by reasonable, Colby meant only a couple of rows of logs tall. He also made sure Linus went inside and retrieved the fire extinguisher. By the time he returned, the late afternoon sun had begun to set in the sky.

It always amazed Colby how early it got dark in the winter months. He'd never thought about in any sort of philosophical way, though. Since Linus explained the pyre, Colby hadn't been able to think about much else.

What did he want to let go of? What did he need to make room for? They were heavy questions, and ones he'd ironically spent the previous night helping answer for his best friend. It seemed too easy to see the answers for Tate.

The question was, why had it taken Colby a trip to Mistletoe Falls to realize he wanted to make some changes as well?

The answer seemed to come in the form of the man who'd bewildered, beguiled, befuddled, and bewitched him from the moment he arrived.

Linus smiled at him when he came out carrying the fire extinguisher. He set it on the ground near the back steps, then continued toward Colby.

"You look confused. Is your eye twitching again? Honestly, Colby."

"My eye isn't twitching. I'm thinking."

"Ha. I thought I smelled smoke. Get it?"

Colby laughed. "I get it, Linus."

"I brought some pens and paper for us to write on. You start with what you're letting go of, and once you give it to the fire to release, you work on what you're making room for. Make sense?"

It did.

Total and complete sense.

And Colby had no idea why.

He sat down on the ground next to Linus as Linus leaned forward and used the candle lighter he'd pulled out of his pocket to light the kindling. It took a few tries to get it going, but then they had a nice, crackling fire started.

"Okay," Linus whispered.

It was the most solemn he'd ever sounded. The intensity of the moment sent a chill down Colby's spine. He put pen to paper and made a list of the things in his life he wanted to let go of. It wasn't a long list. Neither was Linus's apparently. He folded his paper several times then fed it to the flames.

Colby did the same, closing his eyes and picturing himself letting go of all the stress and giving himself time to find a family of his own. Like Linus, he'd had envy in his heart for his chosen family. He loved Tate like a brother and wanted all the Bixbys to have the most amazing life. They loved him like one of their own.

But he wanted more. He wanted someone to call his own, but he couldn't do that if he didn't make time. So that's what he added to his list next, for things he wanted to make room for in his life.

Love.

A family.

A connection to something other than his job.

He folded the page and added it to the flames at the same time Linus added his own. Sparks flew and the fire surged into the air. They might as well have thrown gasoline on it.

"Linus, quick. Grab the fire extinguisher."

Linus grabbed his arm and forced him to stay still. "Colby, wait."

Colby waited, staring into Linus's eyes as the flames continued to grow beside them. Linus's eyes glowed from the light of the fire, and then, in a sign not even Colby could ignore, a little piece of mistletoe drifted away from the fire and danced above Linus's head.

"Linus." Colby leaned in and brushed his lips over Linus's, once then again. "What's happening?"

"Magic," Linus sighed.

He deepened the kiss and Colby pulled him closer. He couldn't say how long the kiss lasted, but the flames had died down when they finally leaned back.

Funny thing, though.

The flames were pretty much gone.

But Linus was still glowing.

Colby closed his eyes, then opened them again.

Yep. Still glowing. It somehow made him even more gorgeous than before.

And it wasn't only Linus. After a moment, more glowing appeared around them. Linus didn't seem to notice.

But Colby? Well, he noticed everything.

"Linus," Colby said, reaching for his hand and squeezing it tight. "I think you just decorated the backyard for Easter. And by the way, you're glowing."

Linus's eyes widened and he jerked his head around. Bunnies and eggs surrounded them in what would have been a glorious display...at the right time of year.

"Dag nab it!" Linus jumped to his feet as more eggs appeared. Then actual bunnies popped into existence and hopped around them.

Matilda bleated, and Colby hurried to free her from her lead. She had on a bunny costume, complete with ears, and she was less than impressed.

"Oh no. Oh no. What have I done?" Linus spun in a circle, looking at the chaos that surrounded them.

Colby tugged his phone out of his pocket and speed dialed his best friend. Tate answered, sounding a little breathless and a lot annoyed. "I'm busy."

"Okay, but considering Linus is glowing and creating bunnies out of thin air, I thought Eldon might want to call a family meeting. We need some help. And Tate? I think you have some explaining to do."

Tate groaned, and not in a good way, before ending the call.

Colby carried Matilda over to Linus and placed her in his arms. It seemed to calm him a little as he cuddled her close. Then he took the fire extinguisher and doused the remains of the pyre.

Linus still had his glow on when Colby finished putting the fire out and returned to his side.

"Linus, sweetheart, look at me." Linus looked up at Colby with his blue eyes glowing and sparks shooting out of his fingers. "What do you call a chicken at the North Pole?"

Linus wrinkled up his nose and gave Colby a less than impressed look. "What?"

"Lost," Colby said.

Linus's eyes widened, and then he burst into laughter. Colby pulled him close and began humming his favorite Christmas song. The glowing continued, but the bunnies began to disappear. The more Colby sang, the more the decorations returned to normal.

By the time Linus's cousins arrived, there were only a few dozen eggs and four or five bunnies left to deal with. Even Matilda's costume had transformed back into her jingle bell harness.

"I hereby request a family meeting," Colby said. "I have questions."

Nyall looked around in a panic. "But Colby, the light parade. We have to get into our costumes and man the booths. We're already running late, and we have to deal with..." Nyall waved his arm around the backyard.

"After the parade," Tate said. "We'll all sit down and talk."

Everyone agreed and the cousins got to work. Nyall and Eldon turned their attention to the bunnies while Oberon focused on the remaining eggs. And of course, they all began to glow as they did their thing.

Once they'd finished, all evidence of Easter vanished.

Linus let out a sigh of relief before shoving Matilda into Colby's arms. "Oh no! We've got to hurry. Don't just stand there, Colby. Move!"

Considering Colby had no idea what he was supposed to do, he followed Linus into the Inn. All of the cousins went to the front closet and pulled out matching elf costumes.

Elves.

Holy magic of Christmas.

They were *elves*.

It explained everything.

"They aren't elves," Tate whispered. "I can see what you're think-ing. And that is absolutely all I can say upon pain of death. And I do mean that literally. Apparently, there are these guys called hell...actually, I can't tell you that either. We'll talk later."

The cousins ran around the Inn, getting changed and gathering what they needed for the night's work. Miles, Tate, Aaron, and Colby stood awkwardly in the lobby waiting for them to get ready.

"Welcome to the family?" Miles said breaking the ice. "I think?"

"Sounds about right." Aaron looked around at the lobby, pointing out a couple Easter eggs still dangling where ornaments should be. "We should probably fix that."

"You've always been my family," Tate added while the other two tried to find all the hidden signs of Easter. "So, you know. Love you and all that stuff."

"Very helpful, Tate," Colby said.

"You should bring Matilda with us to walk the light parade route," Miles suggested. "I'll have my daughter, Holly, and our pups, Ivy and Jingle. It'll be good experience for her."

"Walk...Matilda."

Miles glanced at Aaron and Tate. "Is he in shock? I mean, I know when Oberon blurted it out to me...oh, but he doesn't know—"

"He's seen things," Tate explained. "His lawyer brain is working. He gets weird when he's thinking. It's all the logic required for him to do his job. You should have seen the proposal he put together for the ways I could be with Eldon but still support my family business. It was a hundred and thirty pages long and had appendixes."

"Whoa," Aaron said. "Next time I need research help on a story, I know who to call."

The cousins reappeared in their elf costumes before Colby could defend himself. Linus took him by the arm and they followed the others outside. Linus kissed his cheek before handing him Matilda's leash.

The next thing he knew, he was walking down the block with Miles and Holly and their dogs. Then Tate appeared beside him with steaming mugs of cocoa that he passed to each of them.

"I'm trying to watch my sugar intake," Colby said right before taking a big gulp and chomping on a few marshmallows.

"Start after Christmas. This cocoa is too good to miss."

Colby couldn't argue the point. He glanced at Tate, then to Linus, and back to his best friend. "I think...."

"Yeah, buddy. I know."

"But how...I just...."

"We know," Miles said. He put his arm around Colby's shoulders. "You just need to make like a Christmas stocking and hang in there."

Tate snorted. "Good one. I'm using that on Eldon. The puns make him crazy."

"Daddy! May I go help Obie work? He's passing out candy canes."

"Go ask if it's okay. We'll wait."

Miles held on to both Ivy's and Jingle's leashes as Holly ran over to one of the decorated booths that raised money for local charities. Oberon stood in his elf costume and scooped Holly up into his arms the moment she ran over to him.

"There were bunnies," Colby said once the little ears were out of hearing distance. "*Magic* bunnies. Why are you acting like everything is normal? And why are Oberon and Holly so cute together? It's ridiculous. And I have a pet goat."

Matilda bleated her agreement.

"And you have a Linus." Tate's point seemed to be the most important of all.

Colby smiled, remembering the warmth of the fire and heat of the kiss he'd shared with Linus. "Yeah. That's...unexpected. I didn't know I needed a Linus."

"Tell me about it," Aaron said. He joined them carrying a small plate of cookies. He bent over and fed one to Ivy and another to Jingle before looking at Miles. "Are these Matilda safe? I brought her one too."

"They are," Miles said before turning to Colby. "Nyall started a pet treat line. We consulted on the recipes."

"Is it okay if I give one to Matilda?" Aaron asked.

Colby glanced down at the little goat and nodded. She demolished the treat in three seconds flat. "Can goats be trained?" Colby asked.

Miles laughed. "Depends on the goat."

After working their shifts at the light parade, the cousins, their partners, kids, and pets all made their way back to the Inn. Oberon and Miles tucked Holly into bed in the nutcracker suite, Ivy and Jingle snuggled with her.

Linus managed to secure Matilda into a pen in the corner of the cousins' living room with Oberon's help. She had some nice, fresh hay, a potty pad which Colby figured she'd probably eat, and a blanket that would no doubt also be used as a snack.

Everyone seemed too calm and relaxed. Even Linus, who'd picked up some knitting needles and began working furiously on a new project while sending surreptitious glances Colby's way.

"Linus, what are you up to?"

"Hmm? Nothing. Why?"

Colby gave him a look. "Linus."

"I'm sitting here waiting on you to unleash the kraken, Colby. We both know you're going to talk for three hours without breathing. Question, though. Are these opening arguments or closing arguments? I started watching some episodes of *Suits* so I could learn more about what you do. Also, do you have a secretary? Asking for reasons."

Aaron and Miles both cackled. Tate shoved his face into a pillow, not that it hid his laughter at all.

Linus's cousins all looked at Colby with interest, like they expected him to have a reasonable answer to such a ridiculous line of questioning. "I do corporate law."

"Uh-huh," Linus nodded, his needles moving furiously.

"I think he's most interested in the secretary question," Tate said before falling into Eldon's lap laughing.

"Of course I have a secretary. And two paralegals. What does that have to do with why there were bunnies in the backyard and why you were glowing and why I think I'm in love with you after knowing you for like a week and not even kissing you until today!"

"You love me?" Linus asked.

He immediately began glowing.

"Aww," Nyall said. "This is my favorite glow up yet. Our Linus finally found his mate."

Aaron tugged a handkerchief out of his pocket and passed it to Nyall.

"Glow up?" Colby asked. "Wait...mate?"

"Mate, comma, fated," Tate said. "It means you're meant to be. He's your one true love and you're his."

Colby blinked and turned to his best friend. "And you believe this?"

"You don't?"

Colby opened his mouth, then closed it again. Linus's needles continued their clicking, drawing his attention. "Are you making me another sweater?"

"Of course. What did you think I was doing? Oh, dear. Your eye is twitching again. Miles, would you mind taking a look at his eye? It keeps doing that, and then he gets this vein in his forehead. I'm worried he's going to have a stroke or something."

Tate laughed so hard he fell off the couch. Colby was tempted to kick him in the nads but managed to refrain.

"He's fine. It happens to lawyers when they're thinking," Miles explained. "I've seen it all the time."

Colby turned to Miles and shot him a look. "Oh really. All the time?"

"All the time," Miles answered. Then he had the audacity to wink.

"Colby, just out of curiosity, do you *need* a secretary and two paralegals? Because on *Suits*—"

"I will not now or ever have an affair with my secretary or my paralegals. I'm a one-person guy, Linus. And you're my person. So, stop worrying. And please tell me those aren't baby goats you're adding to the sweater."

"They aren't baby goats," Linus parroted.

"Pretty sure it's *a* baby goat. Singular," Eldon explained. "It's Matilda."

The vein in Colby's forehead began to throb.

"Oh, I see what you mean, Linus." Miles stood up and moved in front of Colby. "That vein is a bit worrisome. We should probably check his blood pressure."

"Or someone could explain to me what in the tiny Dancer is going on here?"

"Was that a pun?" Aaron asked. "It wasn't very clear."

"He can do better," Tate said. "He needs practice."

Colby flung his hands up in the air and walked over to Matilda's pen. She bleated at him, so he picked her up and began pacing around the room. He stopped in front of Aaron.

"You. When did you arrive in Mistletoe Falls?"

"November 30."

"And when did you realize Nyall was your mate?"

"The moment he fell on top of me."

"Fell on...never mind. And did he glow and do magic?"

"So much magic. Cookies decorated to look like me, gingerbread houses built themselves, and our loft kept blowing lights. Powerful magic. You should have seen what happened the first time we—"

Nyall slapped his hand over Aaron's mouth to shut him up.

"Uh-huh." Colby moved to Miles next. He put Matilda in the vet's lap before crossing his arms over his chest. "And how about you?"

"Well, I mean, it just kind of happened. One minute I was a single dad moving to a small town to start a new life with my daughter and our goofy dog, and the next I was head over heels in love with the handyman I met the day I arrived."

"Interesting." Colby turned to Tate. "Stop laughing or I'm calling your mother and telling her that you spiked the eggnog when we were in high school so you and your siblings could all get tipsy."

"You wouldn't."

"You know I would. You will be in *so* much trouble."

"I'm thirty-three years old, Colby. My mother doesn't—"

"Yes, she does," Eldon interrupted. "He'll stop laughing. This isn't funny, Tate. Your best friend found the love of his life. We should be celebrating with him and not laughing at him. I should call your mother and tell her that."

"Stop threatening me with my mother. She'll be here in a week!"

"Technically six days," Colby said. "I arranged for the family to arrive on Friday so we could all spend a long weekend together."

Tate shook his head. "When did you have time to do that?"

"I make time. Now, where was I?"

"I believe you were going to confess your undying love to Linus," Nyall said, still sniffing into the handkerchief Aaron had given him. "It's so romantic."

Colby glanced at Linus, who looked up at him with those big blue eyes, his knitting needles clacking out a rhythm that matched the throbbing in Colby's temple. He was absolutely, completely, head over heels in love with a magical being who drove him crazy in the best possible way.

He knelt in front of Linus and put his hands over the needles, forcing them to still. "You're just too good to be true," Colby sang softly, "I can't take my eyes off of *Yule*."

Linus got a bit teary and put his knitting aside. "You're so *pine...* and you're *mine*."

He moved off the chair and onto Colby's lap, wrapping his arms around Colby's neck as he went. Colby squeezed him tight. "This is a definite *Claus* for celebration."

Everyone laughed.

Linus released Colby from his hug and leaned in to give him a sweet kiss. "The goddesses truly graced me with your *presents*."

And Colby couldn't agree with anything more than that.

8

LINUS

Linus squeezed his eyes shut and waggled his fingers at the guest room. He opened one eye and sighed. "It didn't work."

"That's because the room is perfect as it is," Colby said.

"You think everything I do is perfect," Linus added.

Colby coughed and Linus turned to check on him. He stood behind Linus with Matilda cradled against his chest. They had on their matching Winter Solstice outfits and looked precious. Linus might have squeezed in enough time to make one for himself as well. It was their first solstice as a family, after all. He had to go all out.

"But I really wanted to make it special. These are our final guests of the year. I can't seem to get my glow on, though." Linus wiggled his fingers at the room again and tried staring really hard and focusing. No glow.

"If your magic isn't working, that means the room doesn't need to be changed. Besides, I'm still not sure how moons and stars are holiday decor. I thought we had another bunny incident on our hands, but I don't know. This seems right."

"Are you sure? Because this is what happened when I came in to clean the room after the previous guests departed. Just poof. New room, new theme. It's very pretty, though."

"I'm sure they'll love it. Now quit fussing and come downstairs. The guests should be here any minute. Once we get them checked in, we need to take Matilda for her walk. It's going to be a long night, so I want to be sure she gets plenty of exercise so she doesn't destroy something while we go do our solstice thing."

Linus glanced around the room once more before nodding and closing the door behind him. "I think I have everything ready for the extended family to come too. It's always been just me and my cousins for Christmas. I don't even know what to think about how much our family grew this year. Aaron's parents are coming in Friday. Tate's whole family is arriving Friday as well. It's going to be chaos."

"And you will love every second of it."

"I will," Linus said with a dreamy sigh. "Do you think we have enough presents? I made sure we had something for everyone, plus the stockings, but I'm just not sure—"

"Linus, between you and Eldon, I've opened more boxes this week than I have my entire life. There are plenty of presents. That's not why everyone is coming anyway. They're here to get to know the newest members of the family."

"Well...I suppose. Did I tell you I made everyone a stocking? I even put a lump of coal in Greg's at Tate's request. Of course, I didn't tell Tate that it's actually dark chocolate. I'm not that mean."

Colby grinned. "He'll love it. You're very thoughtful, even when you're nervously babbling about something you shouldn't be worried about at all. They're going to love you as much as I do."

Linus kissed Colby's cheek. "I love you, too. We should do the pyre every year. It really worked for us."

"Linus, I don't think—"

"Oh, Obie said he'd have Matilda's play area built in time for Christmas. Miles said he could wait on some of the house renovations to work on it. Isn't that sweet?"

"It is, but about the—"

"I can't believe how much there is to learn about baby goats. I mean, it probably would have been best to adopt one of those poor kittens or puppies, but I couldn't abandon Matilda to such a cruel fate, now could I?"

Having a pet goat was a lot more work than Linus thought it would be. He'd done several hours of research and spoken to several goat specialists over the past few days. With Miles across the street to help guide them, Linus knew they'd be able to give her an amazing life.

As long as she stopped eating everything in sight. The silly, perfect goat.

Linus hummed a Christmas carol as they went back to the lobby. They timed their arrival just right, their new guests came in moments later.

Linus beamed at them. "Dr. Jerrick! Mr. Jerrick. We're so glad you made it safely. Welcome to the Tinseled Inn."

"Thank you. But please, call me Vaughn. This is my husband, Sam. And...is that a goat?"

"Yep," Linus said. "That's our Matilda. We're going to be taking her on her afternoon walk soon, but we wanted to be sure to be here to greet you."

Vaughn grinned. "I'm a vet, by the way. Matilda looks very healthy and happy, even if I wasn't expecting her to be a pet at an inn."

"We weren't expecting her either. But she's the best pet for us," Colby said. "When she's not trying to eat the yellow snow, that is. I keep trying to tell her, but she just won't listen."

Vaughn and Sam laughed and joined hands.

"Reminds me of our kids when they were growing up. You never know what they're getting up to."

"It's so true," Linus said. "How many kids do you have?"

"Six," Sam said. "They're all grown now, though. Now we get to spoil our grandkids rotten. We snuck away for a couple of days before Christmas so we could have some time alone before the invasion begins."

"Same here," Linus said. "Our whole family arrives on Friday. It's going to be chaos. You have the Inn to yourselves, though. Well, except for Colby, Matilda, and me."

"It sounds perfect. I'm sad we won't be able to see the light parade," Sam said. "But we have to get home early Friday."

"It's okay. We celebrate the Winter Solstice as well, so the town square will have some new things to explore tomorrow. Here's a discount card for my cousin Eldon's shop, and one for my other cousin Nyall's bakery. Enjoy yourselves and don't hesitate to let us know if you need anything."

"This is just what we needed," Vaughn said, pressing a kiss to Sam's temple.

Linus grinned. "Let me show you to your room. Also, we occasionally have dogs in the house, so they might react to...you know."

Vaughn froze. "Pardon?"

Colby looked up in confusion as well.

"The wolf thing," Linus whispered. "And since you're an alpha... well, you know...dogs are sometimes an issue. I don't think we'll have a problem, though."

"Wolf thing?" Colby asked.

"I'll tell you later," Linus said shooting him a glare. "Don't be rude. Alphas can be really cranky."

"What's an alpha?"

Linus tried to use his magic to zip Colby's mouth shut but it didn't work. The last thing they needed was a cranky alpha wolf on their hands.

"Oh goodness," Sam said. "Another newbie, huh?"

"Quite new," Linus said. "He has a lot to learn. It's been quite the holiday season."

"Wait? There are things other than sprites?" Colby asked.

"Oh, *sprites*," Sam exclaimed. "I wondered what you were, but I didn't want to be rude and ask. We studied sprites with our kids when they were younger. Your magic is so special. What a delightful surprise. I knew we found Mistletoe Falls for a reason."

"Everyone does," Colby says. "It's...well, part of the magic."

Linus beamed at Colby, his earlier comments forgiven. "Now, let's get you to your room so you can explore the town to your heart's content."

Vaughn and Sam followed Linus up the stairs and down the hall to their room. After giving them a brief tour, Linus returned downstairs, beaming a smile.

"That explains the moon and stars. Our first alpha wolf shifter. I can't believe it. And his mate is *human*. I can't wait to tell my cousins about this."

Linus went to the front closet and pulled out his coat. They'd had a few inches of snow the night before which added to the beauty of the town's holiday appearance.

"Colby, what are you waiting for? Get your bells shaking. We need to get Matilda walked."

Colby shook his head as he pulled his leather jacket on over his newest sweater from Linus. "I don't think I asked enough questions," Colby said.

"Trust me, you asked enough." Linus wrapped his arms around Colby and pulled him close. "Oh look. We're under the mistletoe. How convenient."

Colby leaned in and kissed Linus deeply before plucking his Santa hat off and putting it on his own head. "When we get home later, I want to make a few special *Santa*-mental memories with you. And I plan to leave on the hat."

The suggestive wink that followed had all sorts of amazing ideas flowing through Linus's head. Linus shivered. "Promise?"

Colby grinned and grabbed Linus's hand, threading their fingers together as they walked outside and let Matilda wander. To neither of their surprise, she went straight to the tree they'd covered with edible ornaments for the neighborhood animals.

Colby had done way too much research on Yule traditions and had kept Linus's crafty fingers busy during the past few days. They even added a few treats for Linus's nemeses—the squirrels. It turned out the tree he'd been attempting to cut down had their winter nest inside of it. It was no wonder they'd pelted him with acorns.

After letting Matilda snack, they walked to the town square where all of the tourists oohed and ahhed over Matilda. She only bit one of them, and that was only because he had a little bit of marsh-mallow on his mitten. She really was the sweetest thing.

Matilda was tired by the time they made it back to the Inn. Linus made everyone a big dinner that would keep them going for the long night ahead. His cousins and their mates all showed up and they gathered for their first meal of the magical new year.

Linus lit several candles down the center of the table, providing the only light for their meal. It was more symbolic than anything else, but Linus loved eating by candlelight, especially during Yule when light officially began to return after the longest night of Winter Solstice.

Their traditions weren't the same as the ones their mates were used to, so much of the meal was spent explaining their customs. It had been a long time since Linus had really thought about them, so it was a sweet moment to share with Colby.

Especially since Colby always asked so many questions, making sure he understood everything clearly. He didn't want to make a mistake, which was silly really, as he couldn't. The goddesses weren't that picky about those learning the old ways.

It was the thought that counted, after all, and Colby would no doubt do his best.

They chatted for hours, long past the time when Holly, Ivy, Jingle, and Matilda were fast asleep. Miles had sweet-talked Gloria to stay at the Inn with them, while they bundled up and headed to the town square.

Every year, the giant spruce stood as a symbol of their belief in the magic they'd been gifted, and every year they celebrated on Winter Solstice by pouring their magic into it. The new decorations would remain until the end of Yule.

"Is anyone else wondering what's going to happen?" Nyall asked softly as he held tightly to Aaron's hand.

"Me," Miles whispered. "I'm nervous and excited."

"Okay, cousins," Oberon said. "You *snow* the drill."

Linus took a deep breath and squeezed Colby's hand a little tighter. "On your marks, get set...Glow!"

What happened next brought tears to Linus's eyes. Not only did the famous Mistletoe Falls spruce light up, but so did the entire town square and beyond. Decorations formed before their eyes, more beautiful and plentiful than they'd ever been before.

Magic rose up within him and went out into the world. Just the way it had been in the old days: strong and bright, reassuring and full of hope.

Linus looked at Colby, whose smile glowed as brightly as the magic surrounding them. He couldn't believe how much the goddesses had blessed him. Blessed them all. Their lives were just starting together, new beginnings for the beginning of the magical year.

When the glow faded, Linus trembled and wrapped his arms around Colby's waist. "That was...."

"*Tree*-mendous," Colby said.

"Yeah, it really was," Linus agreed. "Let's go home."

Nyall and Aaron stayed behind at the bakery while Eldon and Tate decided to spend the night at the loft. Miles and Oberon walked back to the Inn with Linus and Colby, where they gathered up the sleeping members of their family and took them all across the street.

Linus went to the back door once they'd left. Colby followed behind with a puzzled frown.

"It's here," Linus said. "Every year."

"What?"

"The Yule log. We don't know who leaves it, but it appears every year on Winter Solstice."

"I read about this," Colby said. "It has to burn all night, right."

Linus nodded. "And we'll light it from a piece of last year's log. It's very powerful magic."

Colby didn't question it. He simply lifted the heavy log and carried it up to the living room to the only log-burning fireplace in the Inn.

They built the fire together, layering kindling under the log. Linus couldn't help but laugh as he glanced at his mate. "I still can't believe you thought I would barbecue Matilda. I'll never get over the horror."

"And you'll never let me live it down. It's fine. What did I know then?"

"Nothing."

Colby brushed a bit of ash from the fireplace and brushed it on Linus's nose. "It really *soots* you."

Linus groaned. "Take that one back. So bad."

"I will if you'll make me some cocoa."

"That can be arranged. Stay here and make sure the log stays burning."

"I'm on it."

Linus hurried downstairs and gathered snacks and drinks for the long night ahead. When he returned, he froze in his tracks. He only just managed to not drop the tray by magically floating it to a table, which he hadn't even known he was capable of doing.

Why the sudden shock?

Because Colby had used his absence to strip down to a pair of boxers. A nutcracker was very strategically placed, its open mouth bulging due to the gift beneath. And Linus had every intention of enjoying his present.

"You said we had to stay up all night," Colby said.

Linus gulped as Colby moved forward, mischief and heat in his gaze.

"Guess what, Linus?"

"W-what?"

"I don't think that's gonna be a problem."

Wishing *elf* and safety to everyone this season and beyond.

Happy Holidays
~Macy

Join Macy's Moonlighters [http://readerlinks.com/l/1828821] to stay up to date on the latest news and releases from Macy and find other readers to talk to about Macy's books.

Keep in touch with Macy Blake!

Join Macy's newsletter

http://readerlinks.com/l/1633213

ABOUT THE AUTHOR

Macy Blake believes in unicorns and fairies, in moonbeams and stardust, and that happily ever after comes in all colors of the rainbow. She loves to lose herself in paranormal romance, living vicariously through her favorite sexy fictional heroes.

These days you can often find her pounding away at the keyboard, trying to capture the magic of her own worlds while arguing with her feisty German Shepherd, Minerva, and her adorable pound puppy, Pomona.

Visit Macy's website
www.macyblake.com

Join Macy's newsletter
http://readerlinks.com/l/1633213

Macy's Moonlighters Facebook Group
http://readerlinks.com/l/1828821

facebook.com/macy.blake.1042

instagram.com/authormacyblake

bookbub.com/authors/macy-blake

amazon.com/author/macyblake

Co-written with Charlie Cochet

Triad of Magic

Magical species should never mix...but when a mage and alpha werewolf find themselves bound together, their forbidden attraction becomes a magic all of its own.

Stand Alones

Diagnosis Wolf

Born This Way

DID YOU KNOW?

If you own a book or borrow it through Kindle Unlimited, you can get Whispersynced audiobooks at a discounted price.

The Chosen One • Hellhound Champions

Magical Mates • Chosen Champions

Made in the USA
Middletown, DE
12 January 2023

22003577R00066